Heart of Stone

Book Three : Langdon Trilogy

By

Susan Elle

For

Ursula Publishing UK

Heart of Stone

Book Three : Langdon Trilogy

Text Copyright © 2015

By Susan Elle

Ursula Publishing UK

Cover Photograph
© /Dreamstime.com

ISBN 978-1-910753-23-1

Other Books by Susan Elle

The Sara Colson Trilogy includes
Sara's Child
Sara's Loss
Sara's Shame
All the above also available as audio books.

Catherine Colson-Sayers Investigations
CCS Investigations : Bk 1 : Missing
CCS Investigations : Bk 2 : The Chosen
CCS Investigations : Bk 3 : Travis
CCS Investigations : Bk 4 : Deleted
CCS Investigations : Bk 5 : Mind Games, due out end
Aug 2015, twice the length of previous books.

Tempest
Broken

Love, Lies & Consequences Trilogy
Love : Bk1
Lies : Bk2
Consequences : Bk3

Langdon Trilogy
Heart & Home : Bk1
Heart of a Lion : Bk2
Heart of Stone : Bk3
www.susan-elle.com

Table of Contents

Chapter One   5

Chapter Two   13

Chapter Three   23

Chapter Four   31

Chapter Five   41

Chapter Six   49

Chapter Seven   60

Chapter Eight   71

Chapter Nine   81

Chapter Ten   90

Chapter Eleven   99

Chapter Twelve   111

Chapter Thirteen   123

Chapter Fourteen   135

Chapter Fifteen   148

Chapter Sixteen   161

Chapter Seventeen   171

Chapter Eighteen   179

Chapter Nineteen   186

Chapter Twenty   200

Chapter Twenty-One   211

Chapter Twenty-Two   218

Chapter Twenty-Three   227

Chapter Twenty-Four   240

Chapter Twenty-Five   246

<u>CHAPTER ONE</u>

She was driving him crazy. Chad had done everything he could think of to get through to her, but Fallon Craemer was a woman without equal in the stubborn department.

Damn it, I left didn't I, gave her the room she said she needed to think clearly? Though what the hell there was to think through is still a mystery to me!

Even then she berated me for going. How was I to know she'd think I'd left her for good? Women!

I can't remember the amount of times she's told me she loves me, then I ask her to marry me and the woman goes bat shit crazy!

I know she wants to travel, see the world and drink it

all in – so why can't we do that together...after we're married?!

Hammering the keyboard of his laptop in a bedroom he's turned into an office, Chad tried to keep his mind on his work but didn't get very much further before saving it and shutting down.

He was still chuntering to himself when he bumped into Pam at the bottom of the stairs where they collided heavily.

"Ooph!" Pam's breath was knocked out of her as strong hands gripped her shoulders to prevent her falling to the floor.

"God damn it – sorry...sorry, Pam – I didn't see you there," Chad apologised quickly. "Are you ok?"

She was just about to answer him when Matt walked in the front door and lifted a brow at their close proximity.

Pam blushed and straightened her skirt before giving her new husband a hesitant smile. "Neither of us was looking where we were going..." she chuckled nervously "...and being a good bit smaller than Chad, I almost got flattened."

Giving his brother a reproachful frown, Matt walked to Pam and put a supportive arm around her waist. "Are you sure you're alright? Come on, I'll make you a cup of tea," he offered while guiding her through to the kitchen.

"I'm going for a walk," Chad huffed before closing the front door behind himself.

The farm was especially lovely in summer and Chad walked through the beef herd without the slightest concern. Stopping to look at one or two more closely, he gently scrubbed his hand over their rough hides and finished with a rub on the forehead.

The herd was trusting and knew Chad well – a group started walking towards him in hopes of food.

"Good job I filled my pockets," he told them as he held his palm out and shared the food he had on him between them. When the pushing and shoving got a little too boisterous, Chad emptied the last of the feed on the ground and walked on.

A couple of the more hopeful ones followed Chad for a few paces, but when he didn't so much as turn back to them they stopped and settled for the lush grass beneath their hooves.

Striding out on long legs, Chad kept going until he came to the old Mason farmhouse. He'd debated renovating it when first they had bought the farm from the Mason's, but had decided that demolition made more sense.

Still, he couldn't deny it had come in handy as storage

for a while. Now it was all but falling down.

A very old, and he was sure, very dangerous wood veranda surrounded the front and sides of the house.

They had decking even before it was called decking – old Joe loved to sit out here with his wife in the warmer evenings. He was devastated when Joyce died – I can't imagine what losing someone you've loved all those years would feel like, but it didn't take him long to follow her.

Walking the perimeter, Chad was careful not to step up on the rotted wood, mindful that he might fall through it.

The rocking chairs still moved occasionally, if the wind was strong enough, and had caused Chad to pause a moment when he'd first seen it happen.

The warm air was still just then and Chad moved to the back of the house, looking for signs of anyone trespassing.

The murderer of 4 women was still on the loose and Chad was looking for any signs of an intruder.

I need to get this land cleared, the damn weeds are nearly up to my waist in places!

He continued round the back of the house and looked for signs of a disturbance, but didn't see anything unusual.

I need to round up all this equipment too, Chad decided, looking at the old scythe laying on the ground.

I can't believe Joe used that right up till he died – he lived in the past, wouldn't even loan our combine harvester to bring the crops in.

Entering the barn, Chad came to a sudden stop – there were definite signs of an intruder here.

That's fresh hay, he observed, looking at a thick pile of it that appeared to have been slept on. Chad moved further into the old barn, his eyes moving quickly to search the shadows for anyone still lurking around.

Jesus, I told Jackson not to try challenging anyone he found while on his own and I'm doing exactly that!

It made him angry to feel threatened on his own land, if there was a vagrant hanging around, murderer or not, he would probably regret meeting Chad in his current mood.

Having checked every nook and cranny, Chad went outside to continue his search.

An ancient tractor was parked beside the barn and Chad glanced at it curiously. *What the hell is that?!*

There was a tin box on the seat of the tractor. *Looks like Joyce's tea-caddy – I'm sure I remember seeing it in her kitchen. So what's it doing here?*

He moved forward to pick it up and tugged the lid open. *Jewellery! A ladies watch, a couple of necklaces and a ring. These don't look like the sort of thing Joyce would have worn, and even if they did belong to Joyce what are they doing out here?*

It was busy on the farm, Jackson was caught up feeding the live-stock, and his father and Matt were heaving sacks of feed into the store.

I suppose Chad's writing his next best seller, Jackson chuckled to himself as he drove away with another load of feed. *Can't imagine doing anything like it myself, but Chad seems to be making a decent living at it.*

It took Jackson a while to distribute the feed and give the cattle a check over, then he took the tractor to reconnoitre the outbuildings.

Because of the farm's size it had feed stores dotted around to make the process of feeding the cattle easier. There was no point going all the way back to the main store every time he ran out, that would just waste man hours and fuel going to a fro.

Some of the buildings were little more than large sheds, others were full sized barns that had been saved from when that particular piece of land had belonged to the previous farmer.

It took quite a while to inspect each building to Jackson's satisfaction, but so far he hadn't found any sign of someone using them as temporary lodgings.

Then he came across a carrier bag that originated

from the village store. It was unlikely to have blown there as it had a couple of empty bottles inside.

Empty beer bottles – there's no one who should be on this farm who would drink beer out in the fields, Jackson told himself as he looked into the carrier bag.

He was careful not to touch the bottles themselves – if they did belong to the man being hunted for the murder of 4 women, Jackson didn't want to contaminate any evidence the police might be able to get from them.

Securing the bag in the cab of the tractor, Jackson continued on his way to inspect the Mason farm.

The Mason's had been very old – too old to take care of the property or make a proper living off the land. The outbuildings were barely standing up and the house wasn't much better.

Poor sods couldn't afford to take on help, it must have been galling to see your life's work crumbling before your eyes. Still, old Joe and Joyce got to die at home on the farm – they'd have hated being cooped up in some nursing home – the outdoors was all they'd ever known.

Starting with the barns, Jackson took even more care now that he suspected someone of being around. It was one thing checking just in case, but now he had real evidence of an unauthorised presence on the farm.

It was possible that the carrier bag, and its contents,

had belonged to a vagrant who had wandered harmlessly onto the farm seeking shelter for the night, but Jackson wasn't taking any chances.

The first barn still housed Joe Mason's tools – he seemed to have made a collection of old scythes over the years, but Jackson didn't take the time to examine them.

He could see all of the floor-space clearly, there were no concealed areas where someone might be hiding, so Jackson continued on his way to the second barn.

That one was a whole other prospect, it had been used to store everything you could imagine. Not only farming supplies and necessities, but also household items that were no longer wanted in the main house.

Now this could be a cosy hideaway for a murderer on the run. And what's this, looks like someone laid out fresh hay to sleep on.

There were myriad places that a person could hide in, and Jackson searched them all but found nothing.

If I'm aiming to check all the outbuildings twice a day I'll have to do one round of checks right at the end of the day, otherwise I'll never get any work done.

Dusting himself off, Jackson was about to cross to the main house when something caught his eye. It was Joe's old tractor and someone was lying beside it.

CHAPTER TWO

Approaching cautiously, Jackson looked at the man sprawled face down on the ground and caught his breath in shock. "Chad! What the hell!"

There was a lot of blood on the ground and Jackson wasn't sure if Chad was still breathing. Taking a precautionary look around, Jackson then dropped to his knees to better examine him.

Jesus, I can't feel a pulse – don't be dead, for christ's sake, don't be dead!

Standing, Jackson pulled out his mobile phone and called for an ambulance. "I can't feel a pulse – if there's one there it's too faint to feel it," he told the ambulance dispatcher. He listened for a minute more then said, "I don't think you'd find where we are on your own – tell the ambulance driver to go to the big house on Langdon Farm, I'll phone down and have someone there ready to show them the way up here."

The next call he made was a difficult one and he knew the one after that would be more difficult still. No matter how stubborn and pigheaded Wesley's sister was, Jackson had a suspicion she still loved Chad.

Telling Matt that his brother appeared to be seriously injured was traumatic to say the least. Matt had bombarded him with questions and demanded that he try again to find a pulse.

"It's no good, Matt..." he'd told Chad's brother "...I'm not feeling anything and I can't see any sign of him breathing either." When Matt suggested turning him over, Jackson had told him no. "I could end up injuring him more than he is already..." he'd reasoned "...best let the professionals take care of him, Matt. They should be with you anytime now – you'll need to show them the way up to Mason's farm."

Yes, that had been traumatic alright, but he'd bet a whole years wages that telling Fallon was going to be a hell of a lot worse.

Fallon didn't always carry her mobile around with her, and this was one of those instances when it resided on the kitchen table while she was in her bedroom.

"Fallon, your mobile's ringing," her mother shouted up the stairs. "Do you want me to answer it?"

But Fallon came out of her bedroom and quickly descended the stairs. "I bet that's Fenella — we're arranging a night out with some of the girls," Fallon grinned as she passed her mother in the hallway.

"You be careful — all of you," Mrs Craemer cautioned. "That awful man is still on the loose and Wesley and Chad will skin you alive if you go off on your own again."

Mrs Craemer watched as her daughter picked up the trilling mobile while rolling her eyes at her, then saw the happiness die on her daughter's face and watched as she sank onto a chair as if her legs could no longer hold her up.

Hurrying forward, she put a hand on Fallon's shoulder and asked, "What is it, what's wrong?"

Her thoughts immediately turned to Wesley — had he been in some sort of accident? But as she listened, Mrs Craemer became aware that Fallon was talking to Jackson, one of the workers on Langdon Farm.

"I'll come right away — I know my way to Mason's farm, I'll come there directly," Fallon told Jackson, and ended the call.

"Fallon...?"

Her mother sounded worried and Fallon looked up at

her through tear filled eyes. "It's Chad, Jackson says it looks like he's been attacked - he's waiting for the ambulance to arrive."

"But he's alive...?" Mrs Craemer asked anxiously.

"Jackson didn't say he wasn't so..." Fallon didn't get to finish her thought as the tears began to fall. "I need to go, I need to get to the Mason's farm right away."

But her mother barred her way. "Not on your own, you're not," Fallon's mother stated firmly. "I'll come with you – there might be something I can do to help in any case," and picking up her first aid kit, she followed her daughter out to the car.

Jackson was pacing the ground back and forth, glancing this way and that in case whoever attacked Chad returned. He'd run to the house and fetched out an old blanket – it might be smelly but he didn't think it mattered. Chad was cold to the touch and there was a chill wind blowing now.

Turning at the sound of a car approaching, Jackson was initially disappointed to see that it wasn't the ambulance.

Fallon pulled up next to Jackson and exited the car in a rush, not bothering to close the door behind her. "Where is he...where's Chad?!"

Jackson looked down at his feet to the blanket

covered body and Fallon's gaze followed. He heard her gasp and watched as she dropped to her knees beside Chad.

"Don't move him," Mrs Craemer shouted to her daughter before Fallon could turn him over.

Leaning down to place her lips over his bloody ear, Fallon whispered to him. "I'm here, Chad. Please don't leave me again, I'll do anything you ask if you just stay with me. I'll even marry you and have half a dozen kids, if that's what it takes…just, please…don't leave me," she begged softly.

He didn't move, didn't appear to be breathing, but Chad still had some colour in his lips so Fallon took heart from that and assumed he was still alive.

"The ambulance is here," Jackson announced with no little relief, and watched as it pulled round Fallon's car to stop just feet away. "He's right here…" Jackson told the paramedic that strode towards them "…I covered him over because he was getting really cold, but no one has moved him."

"That's good," the paramedic told them. Then he and another ambulance man bent down to examine Chad.

"Thanks for staying with him," Matt told Jackson as they watched the paramedics at work.

"No problem – I wouldn't have left him on his own no

matter what," Jackson stated firmly. "I found a carrier bag with a couple of empty beer bottles in it just across the next field from here – I've got a feeling we have a visitor in our midst – maybe even a lodger."

"You think he may have attacked Chad?" Matt asked, turning shocked eyes to Jackson.

"I think that's a good bet, yes – though I haven't seen hide nor hair of anyone," Jackson replied, his eyes darting to look in every direction just in case the attacker was watching the scene.

"Ok, I'll be going with Chad to the hospital – you get your dad, and mine, then do a more thorough search for signs of this intruder – and get that bag and its contents to the police," Matt told Jackson before walking over to see Fallon and her mother.

"Oh, Matt." Fallon turned into him and Matt enfolded her in his strong arms to offer comfort. "I can't lose him, Matt – I just can't lose him."

"Chad's more stubborn than the proverbial mule – you won't get rid of him any time soon," Matt told her, hugging Fallon as she wept into his shirt.

I just hope I'm right – my parents will have a hard time dealing with any other outcome. So will I, come to that. When all's said and done, Chad's my brother and I'd do anything in my power to keep him alive!

After fitting a collar around Chad's neck to stabilise his spine, the paramedics loaded him into the ambulance and blue lighted him to the hospital.

Only Matt had been allowed to ride in the ambulance with his brother – Fallon had to get herself to the hospital, but there was no doubt that she would arrive only minutes after the ambulance did.

Matt had implored her not to speed – it wouldn't do any good if they both ended up being admitted as patients.

But Fallon was terrified of never seeing Chad again and once her mother was safely seated in the car next to her, Fallon took off to follow on the heels of the ambulance.

The crew had radioed ahead to let the ER know what was coming in and when they pulled up a small team of doctors and nurses was there to greet them.

The lead paramedic was firing off statistics about Chad's heart rate, blood pressure and a lot of other confusing stuff, but Matt just concentrated on watching Chad as he was quickly wheeled in.

Suddenly a large hand came up, barring Matt's way. "Sorry sir, you'll have to wait out here."

"But, he's my brother," Matt gasped, not wanting to let Chad out of his sight.

Now he knew how Fallon had felt – was he ever going to see Chad alive again?!

Barely five minutes after taking a seat in the waiting room, Matt watched Fallon and her mother enter the accident and emergency department. He got up to greet them and let them know what was going on.

"He never woke up in the ambulance…" he began "…though I kept talking to him the whole time. But the paramedic said that wasn't unusual with such a severe head injury – he wouldn't even give me odds on Chad ever waking up again."

Mrs Craemer guided the pair over to a seating area and told them to sit down. "You two need to think more positively – all this angst might be totally unnecessary. Now then, I don't know about you but I could certainly do with a nice cup of tea – Fallon, Matt?" she asked with a raised brow.

"Not for me," Fallon declined automatically.

"I wouldn't mind a coffee – let me get them, it'll give me something to do," Matt told the older woman.

Taking a seat by her daughter, Mrs Craemer took Fallon's hand in hers and brought it up to her lips. "Pray for him, Fallon – that's all we can do now."

"I've been praying for Chad since the moment I answered that damnable call," Fallon stated harshly. "If only he hadn't gone up there alone — what on earth possessed him to do such a fool thing with a murderer on the loose?!"

Nodding, Mrs Craemer acknowledged the sentiment. "It does seem strange that Chad would take such a risk, but I'm sure he had his reasons."

"That's the trouble with Chad, he always has a reason for doing things his own way!" Fallon erupted and got to her feet. With hands flailing expressively she paced the floor in front of her mother. "When he asked me to marry him I said, let's just wait a while. When I asked him to give me a little time and space when he began badgering me about it, he took off, left me in the dust to pick up the pieces...then he comes back, large as life, and says he was just giving me the space I'd asked for! "

Turning to her mother, Fallon shook her head, her expression one of disbelief. "He was even talking babies. Babies, for christ's sake!"

"Well, I would think that's quite a normal thing to want to iron out," Mrs Craemer reasoned quietly, then watched as her daughter began to bristle.

"And I think not wanting children the moment you get married is quite reasonable," Fallon huffed. "Now the great lummox has gotten himself so badly injured we don't even know if he'll live — well just you wait till he wakes up, I'll tear a strip off him so wide it'll put this head injury to shame!"

Defiant and angry, Fallon turned back to her mother, her bottom lip trembling perilously. Then the damn broke and Fallon cried like her heart would break.

Moments later Matt returned, three hot drinks held on a cardboard box lid. He was shocked to see the state Fallon was in and assumed the worst.

"Dear God, not Chad?!"

His hands began to tremble and Mrs Craemer shot up to take the make-shift tray from him. "No, no, Fallon is getting herself into a tizzy – we haven't heard anything about Chad yet."

Sitting next to Fallon, Matt put a comforting arm round her shoulders and gave her a hug. "Have a drink of tea – I went to the WRVS and asked them to make it just how you like it," he smiled.

"Here you go," Mrs Craemer held out the tea to Fallon and waited while she used a tissue to dry her cheeks.

"I'm sorry, I think it must be the waiting that got to me," Fallon apologised, taking a sip of the tea. "This is good, thanks Matt, sorry I scared you."

CHAPTER THREE

Three cups of tea later, and a lot of pacing back and forth, the A&E consultant came out to speak to Chad's family. The nurse who emerged beside him indicated Matt and the two women with him.

"Hello, I'm Mr Fenton, sorry to meet you under such circumstances. If you wouldn't mind following me we'll have a talk about Mr Langdon's condition," the smiling consultant said.

"Well, at least we know he's still alive," Matt grimaced as they all filed into a small interview room.

The consultant had obviously heard Matt's remark as he began by picking up on it. "The fact that Mr Langdon is still alive is something of a miracle," he began.

Looking at the anxious faces of those facing him, the

consultant went into more detail. "Mr Langdon arrested twice…" he held up a staying hand as Fallon would have jumped in "…but we now have him stabilised. He lost a lot of blood and has received four units of red cells to compensate. But it's the head injury that is our main concern – we've taken Mr Langdon to theatre as the fracture to his skull is very serious and the lacerations to the scalp are full thickness."

He stopped for a moment, assessing how much of the information that he was imparting was actually being taken in. "I don't know if you found the implement used to inflict the injuries, but I'd guess it is metal with some kind of rounded protrusion that caused the skull to fragment in the area where Mr Langdon was bludgeoned."

"Fragmented…what the hell does that mean – his head isn't a bloody eggshell for christ's sake," Matt demanded furiously, his anxiety turning fear to rage.

"In fact, we found two small pieces of skull that had broken away and were lying beneath the scalp, as well as evidence of extensive fracturing," the consultant explained, keeping his voice soft and low but firm.

Fallon looked as if she were about to faint and her mother quickly gathered her daughter to her side.

"Here, sit down before you fall," Mrs Craemer

insisted, pushing her daughter onto one of the chairs provided. The nurse brought over another chair and Mrs Craemer thanked her then took a seat next to Fallon.

"So what you're really saying is, you think he may have suffered some brain damage," Mrs Craemer said as she looked up at the consultant.

"Let's all take a seat and I'll explain exactly what we've found and what we suspect might be the outcome," Mr Fenton told them.

By the time Matt, Mrs Craemer and Fallon walked out of the interview room, they were all feeling less than hopeful of a good outcome for Chad.

"If I ever get my hands on the bastard who did this to him, I'll show him what it's like to be on the receiving end of a good pasting," Matt fumed.

"They said he'd be transferred to ICU when he comes out of theatre... "Mrs Craemer recalled "...perhaps we should find our way to their waiting room, if they have one?"

Just then, Avis Langdon came rushing through the outer doors and into the A&E department.

"Where is he – where's Chad?!" she demanded the second her eyes landed on Matt.

"They've taken him to theatre..." Matt told her "...he's got a badly fractured skull and other injuries."

She looked blank for a moment, then put a hand to her forehead. "I wasn't home – when Jackson came for your father – I was in the village talking with friends."

"Now then, Avis, you can't blame yourself for that," Mrs Craemer assured her. "You've just come back after a year away, of course you've got friends to catch up with. But you're here now, so let's go up and wait for Chad to come out of theatre."

Jackson, Charley and Mac were all out searching the farm for any sign of the intruder. They found footprints in some of the softer ground and followed them.

"No splitting up…" Charley ordered "…we stay in sight of each other at all times. That murdering bastard isn't going to get another of us while I'm around!"

He thought of Chad, his son was fighting for his life and Charley wanted to be with him – but for now, this was more important. If they had a chance to catch the man who'd tried to kill him, they had a duty to at least try.

And what if he's the same man who's been killing women in the area – we need to do what we can as carefully as we can before he gets away.

The police were on their way and had warned Jackson not to tackle the man alone when he'd called them. But the three men had started out immediately, not wanting to give the attacker any more time to slip away.

They walked a meter apart, searching the ground for clues but being careful not to destroy the footprints that could belong to the attacker.

They'd already come across a bloody ball hammer and had left it where it was, carelessly tossed into a long tangle of weeds.

As carefully as they searched, they didn't find anything else, and when the police arrived they told them of their progress.

"The ball hammer is over here…" Charley showed a detective where it lay "…no one has touched it or moved it in any way."

"That's good – Mr Langdon is it?" the detective asked with a curious frown.

"It is – this used to be the Mason's farm, we bought it when it became too much for them to work it. Though old Joe still lived here till he died."

Mac watched as the police interviewed Charley and supposed they'd get around to him and Jackson in time. But now he walked over to his son and clapped him on his back. "I don't want you blaming yourself over this. You did as you were asked – you checked all the outbuilding and this was the last of them – you weren't to know Chad would get here before you and be attacked."

Scuffing the toe of his boots into the ground, Jackson

nodded but didn't look at his father. The fact was, he did feel guilty about Chad's attack, he just couldn't figure out why.

His father was right, he had done as he'd been asked…and why hadn't Chad taken his own advice? He'd insisted that Jackson not try to tackle anyone he came across on his own – the very thing, it appeared, that Chad himself had done with dire consequences.

"I just wish he'd asked me to go with him if he planned to search the Mason place," Jackson finally said. "With both of us here we might even have caught the bastard!"

"Hindsight is always 20:20 vision, son," Mac replied. "I doubt Chad planned to come up here, probably did so on a whim and didn't think it through. Wouldn't be surprised if he hadn't argued with someone – always did take off after a row, even when he was a kid."

The detective had apparently finished with Charley and was making his way towards Jackson and Mac.

"I understand it was you who found Mr Chad Langdon after the attack," the detective said, looking at Jackson as he did so.

"That's right."

"So what can you tell me about it?" the detective asked when Jackson didn't continue.

"Not a lot – I was out checking the outbuildings all over the farm – this was the last port of call and I found Chad already laid on the ground," Jackson recited the story he'd told everyone else.

"Did you see anyone running away from the scene?" The detective was looking at Jackson with an unnerving interest and Jackson noticed it.

"I didn't attack Chad! I don't know who did but I didn't!" Jackson pulled himself up to his full height and his broad chest broadened impressively as he glared down at the detective.

"I don't remember suggesting such a thing," the detective smiled slyly. "Did you see the ball hammer just over there?" the detective asked, pointing to where it lay in a weed bed.

"I took a look after Charley found it – it isn't like anything I've seen in use on the farm," Jackson growled.

Mac shot his son a warning look and Jackson took a long breath to calm himself.

"Thank you for your help, Mr...?"

"The name's Jackson."

"Mr Jackson..." the detective said, mistakenly assuming it was his surname "...we may need to talk to you again at a later date."

Without correcting the detective's mistake, Jackson

gave him a nod then walked over to Charley to see what he wanted to do next.

Mac, however, stayed where he was and gave the detective a meaningful look. "My son is not a violent man, unless he's pushed too far. He's not the one as attacked Chad, and he's not the murderer attacking local women – best you start looking elsewhere for your man, Detective."

CHAPTER FOUR

Fallon sat at Chad's bedside for as long as the nurses would allow. She held his hand and talked to him – though it was more like threatening to give him what for if he didn't hurry and wake up.

Often she just laid her cheek against his hand on the bed and wished it would move, just a finger even. But there was nothing.

The nurses had been very positive – Chad was breathing for himself and holding his own body temperature, all good signs.

His heart rate was a little precarious, sometimes shooting up to alarming levels, at others settling at such a low rate the nurses became concerned.

All in all, Chad was holding his own. *Maybe Matt was right, Chad's too damn stubborn to die!*

"Please wake up…" she asked Chad again "…or just give my hand a squeeze so I know you can hear me."

It was no use, but Fallon wouldn't give up. She got a copy of a newspaper from the visitor's room and read him all of the sporting news. Chad hated sports, especially football, but Fallon deliberately read every word she could find on the subject.

"Now here's a good bit – says Hampton really shot themselves in the foot – scored two own goals and gave away a penalty," Fallon chuckled as she continued to read aloud. "The final score was 3 nil against Hampton – I bet the air in the dressing room was on the blue side when the manager got in there. What do you think?"

Chad actually groaned and Fallon dropped the newspaper in her hurry to stand.

"Chad? Chad…can you hear me – please, my love, open your eyes?!" When they fluttered open Fallon gasped and kissed him enthusiastically, then backed off quickly when he groaned.

"Oh god, did I hurt you?" she asked frantically. "I'll get the nurse…the doctor…someone should come and see to you…"

His eyes closed and Fallon hurried from the room.

"Nurse, Chad opened his eyes, I think he's in pain," Fallon told the nurse who had been in to see Chad earlier.

"I'll be right there..." the nurse told her "...I'm just going to let Dr Plover know."

Fallon rubbed Chad's hands while she continued to speak to him, all of it so much nonsense but she couldn't stand the silence.

Chad didn't open his eyes again until the doctors did a test that Fallon thought was barbaric, but it worked.

Dr Plover pressed his thumb nail into the nail bed of Chad's little finger in order to gain a response.

Chad tried to pull his finger away from whatever was causing him pain and the doctor smiled. "That's a good sign..." Dr Plover smiled over to Fallon in time to see her grimace "...Mr Langdon is no longer comatose – although he isn't yet properly conscious he is responding appropriately to painful stimuli."

"I should think he has enough pain to be going on with," Fallon observed, a tremulous smile showing her relief.

"He's been on intravenous morphine since the operation," Dr Plover told her. "Nurse will monitor his pain levels and up the dose as required. The more conscious Mr Langdon becomes, the more he will be aware of his pain. However, we don't want to give him too much as morphine also has a sedative effect. We'll change him onto something else in due course."

"Two days you've been asleep…" Fallon told Chad when they were left alone again "…and all I get is a groan and a moment with your eyes open. Perhaps I should read you some more football news, that seemed to do the trick last time."

Bending down to pick the newspaper up from under the bed where she'd dropped it earlier, Fallon straightened up to find Chad looking at her.

His head was swathed in bandages, but Fallon touched his cheek as Chad tried to smile.

"You scared me half to death, don't ever do that again," she told him, tears falling onto Chad's cheek as she bent over him.

His conscious episodes were fleeting but Fallon was grateful to see Chad's eyes open now and then, or feel his fingers very gently curl around her own.

His parents and Matt had been in and out during visiting times, but none of them were yet aware that Chad was gradually waking up.

"Chad?" He didn't open his eyes or move his fingers, so Fallon took it that he was asleep and crept out of the room. She spoke to Chad's nurse before leaving the ward to call his parents.

Avis was so relieved to hear that her son had regained consciousness, however briefly, that she was unable to speak and Charley had taken over the conversation.

"Fallon, did I hear right, is Chad awake?" Charley asked cautiously. "He was…he is…well that's great news – I'll call Matt and let him know. We've all been so worried. Bless you for letting us know – tell him we'll all be in to see him tomorrow."

It was almost 10pm when Fallon got back to Chad's room. Avis had come back on the phone and they'd shed a few tears together. Happy ones, this time.

"I've told your parents that you're waking up, Chad. Your mother cried and your dad sounded overjoyed," Fallon told him, though Chad's eyes remained closed. She hoped he was sleeping. "Charley said they'll all be coming in tomorrow – not quite sure who 'all' means, probably just them and Matt…and maybe Pam too."

She really didn't want to leave him, but the nurses had been very tolerant considering they had visiting times that everyone else had to stick to.

"I have to go, Chad. I really don't want to, but I can't push my luck with the nurses any more than I have already. I'll ask if I can come a bit earlier in the morning," she told him. Then she bent closer and kissed his lips gently. "I love you, you mule headed man. You drive me so damn crazy…but I do love you."

His head was fuzzy and his eyelids were as heavy as

lead, but Chad smiled inside. If this was a dream it wasn't half bad, he could have sworn he'd just heard Fallon's voice telling him that she loved him.

He was in and out of consciousness, the dreams not always as the one he'd had about Fallon. Someone was attacking him – it felt like the world had crashed down on his head and then the lights went out.

Had that really happened – Chad couldn't hold on to one thought long enough to make sense of it. When he awoke in the night, the room semi dark with no one around, Chad began to panic.

Where the hell am I? What's going on, why can't I move? His heart rate and blood pressure had spiked alarmingly and a doctor and a nurse came hurrying into the room.

He was thrashing his head from side to side, desperate to…to… He didn't know what he wanted to do, but Chad knew he didn't want to be here, where ever here was!

"Ok, Mr Langdon, just hold still and let us help you," the doctor instructed in a firm but kind voice. "You're in the hospital and we are looking after you. Now try to calm down and we'll explain everything."

The nurse had managed to untangle one of the IV lines and hook it out of the way, the one with the morphine, however, was dangling uselessly off the bed.

"His pain relief is out…" the nurse informed the doctor "…but his fluids line is still intact."

"Ok, no worries, well change him onto NG pain relief with morphine boluses if necessary," the doctor told her. "Now…Mr Langdon, I'm Dr Plover and I've been looking after you since you came out of theatre."

"Theatre…?" Chad's voice was raspy and barely audible, but the doctor was able to make it out.

"Yes, you had to have surgery on your head. Do you remember anything that happened to you – how you got your head injury?" the doctor urged.

Calmer now, Chad frowned as he tried to pull together the shards of memory that only gave him glimpses of something traumatic. "No," he said eventually. "Just feelings, pain, shock…then nothing."

"Not to worry, that's perfectly normal at this stage," the doctor assured him. "Hopefully it will come back to you in time, but it isn't unusual for your brain to block the memory from ever returning. We'll just have to wait and see what happens."

Chad's eyelids still felt heavy, but he had so many questions to ask, he didn't want to fall back into the darkness where he couldn't make sense of anything.

As hard as he struggled against it, Chad felt himself

sink beneath the dark veil of sleep and disturbing dreams.

For the rest of that day Chad was in and out of sleep, his awake times gradually increasing.

"Hello again," Fallon smiled as Chad's eyes flickered open. "I brought you my iPod in so you can listen to some books or music – I doubt you're up to reading an actual book yet," she grimaced in sympathy.

"Thanks – what books did you put on it?"

"A couple of Stephen King's and a small variety of crime and murder novels." Fallon grinned mischievously, "There were a couple of Nora Roberts books on there – I almost left them on but decided you probably weren't into romances."

As expected, Chad frowned disapprovingly. "Not my kind of book, no. Though I hear her JD Robb books are very entertaining and even a bit on the gory side."

"Hmm, I've read all of them – they're quite addictive once you get into the series," Fallon told him. "How's your pain," she asked after noticing him grimace.

"Not too bad," he lied. "No worse than you'd expect after getting your head caved in with a hammer."

"Is that what they told you?" Fallon gasped.

"The police have been in – apparently my dad found a bloody ball hammer nearby where it happened," Chad explained. "The doctor's reckon it fits in with my injuries."

"Then he really meant to kill you," Fallon said, her face paling visibly, the horror mirrored in her eyes.

"Well he didn't do a very good job, so stop thinking about it," Chad ordered, his voice growing stronger. "I'll be out of here before you know it, then we need to talk," he told her ominously.

Fallon frowned and moved her chair closer to the bed, taking his hand. "We could talk now, it's not like anyone is here."

At that moment a nurse came into the room and changed the fluids on his IV line. "How are you doing today, Mr Langdon," the nurse asked as she worked.

"It's Chad, and I'm fine," but he grimaced when a sudden bolt of pain shot through his head on turning to face her.

"Hmm, I'm not so sure about that – I could give you a morphine injection to take the edge off," she offered.

But Chad refused. "I don't want to keep falling asleep and morphine seems to do that to me. I'll be fine as long as I stop moving my head."

The nurse chuckled. "Well, that will work for now but we'll be getting you out of bed later today. I think you might need something before we do that."

"So soon!" Fallon gasped in surprise and concern.

"It's been three days," the nurse said, as if that was

quite long enough. "Apart from his head, Mr Langdon has no other injuries so really needs to get himself moving. Just lying in bed can cause complications that we really don't want to contemplate."

CHAPTER FIVE

After just 6 days Chad was allowed out of hospital, with a warning that he still needed to take things slowly.

Fallon had been so shocked that she'd demanded to speak to a doctor before taking Chad home.

"All of Mr Langdon's responses are appropriate and the injury itself has healed well," Dr Plover assured her. "If you have any concerns, should Mr Langdon exhibit strange behaviours or if his speech becomes slurred, don't hesitate to get back in touch," and he gave her a card with the unit's telephone numbers on it.

"Strange behaviours...slurred speech...?" Fallon could only gape at the doctor.

"We don't expect any of that to occur, but they are signs that other damage is present – damage that isn't apparent at this time," Dr Plover explained. "A build-up of fluid around the brain can cause such symptoms – we would need to know about that as a matter of urgency. Other than that, we would like to see Mr Langdon at the outpatient's clinic in 6 weeks – has nurse given you a letter with the details?"

"Yes…yes," Fallon confirmed hesitantly.

"Don't look so worried, we don't expect there to be any complications – Mr Langdon has had a very lucky outcome considering the attack. He's ready to go home to finish off his recuperation," the doctor smiled as he left.

Going back into Chad's side-room, Fallon looked very formidable as she contemplated the man sat in an armchair on the opposite side of the bed.

"What…?" Chad asked when Fallon continued to frown at him without speaking.

"I'm just working things out in my head," and Fallon nodded as if she'd come to some conclusion. "Wes can stay in your room at the farm and you'll stay in Wesley's at our place – that way I can keep an eye on you."

"What?!" Chad sat upright in his seat. "I don't need you or anyone else keeping an eye on me," he growled angrily. "I'm not a child, I can look after and keep an eye on myself!"

"Did the doctor tell you about the possible symptoms

you might exhibit that could indicate a fluid build-up around the brain?" Fallon asked, hands on hips her expression unyielding.

"Of course, but-"

"But nothing, Chadwick Langdon! You will stay with us and like it – or I swear I'll move into Ashton's room and she can move into mine – whichever way it works, I will be keeping an eye on you!"

Narrowing his eyes, Chad considered arguing the point but could see he'd be wasting his time and energy. And besides, his bloody head was throbbing!

"Jesus, woman – I've never met such a bossy female! Have it your own way..." Chad sat back and closed his eyes "...but don't start complaining when I get on your last nerve because I'll remind you that this was all your idea!"

Satisfied that she had won this round, Fallon was well aware that there would be many more ahead of her. Chad Langdon didn't know how to accept help, and she intended to help him whether he liked it or not!

Charley and Avis came to the hospital with Matt and they all piled into his car to transport Chad to the Craemer's farm.

"This is such a good idea..." Avis enthused during the journey "...I have to admit, I've been worried sick about Chad coming home. Are you sure you'll manage, dear – he can be a bit prickly when he isn't well?"

"Stop talking about me like I'm not here," Chad snapped, and Avis raised a brow at Fallon in an 'I-told-you' manner that caused Chad to frown deeply.

"We'll be fine – won't we?" she demanded of Chad in a menacing tone.

"Oh sure, I'll just smile and be a good little boy," he replied in a too sweet voice.

"Ha! That'll be the day," Fallon chuckled and everyone joined in, much to Chad's chagrin.

Thankfully it wasn't a long journey back to Dersley Dale and the Craemer's farm, or Chad might have been tempted to punch someone!

"Come on, bro'." Matt opened Chad's door and waited for him to climb out of the car. "Just lean on me if you need to."

The look Chad shot him had Matt taking a step back. "I can bloody walk by myself, damn it!"

Holding his hands palms out in defence, Matt said, "Go for it, bro, just don't fall on your face in front of the ladies," Matt smiled, jutting his chin out to indicate the welcoming committee.

Mrs Craemer, Fallon, Pam and even Lizzy were all stood together watching his slow progress.

He wanted to stride into the house as he had done

many times before, but Chad felt dizzy and his head hurt with every footstep that seemed to jolt his brain inside his battered skull.

"It's so good to see you," Sheila Craemer told him as Chad stepped over the threshold into the house. "Hearing what happened to you gave me such a fright."

Chad managed a sincere smile, knowing that Mrs Craemer would have worried about him every bit as much as his own mother had. "Takes a bit more than a couple of taps with a hammer on the head to take me down," Chad joked smoothly.

He heard Lizzy gasp and gave her a wink.

"It was a bit more than a tap as I heard it," Mrs Craemer frowned. "Are you sure you should be out of the hospital – it seems a bit soon to me?"

"That exactly what I said!" Fallon stood with her hands on her hips and gave Chad an 'I told you so' look.

"It's not like I signed myself out," Chad protested. "The doctors seemed to think I'd recover better at home. Apparently, the longer you stay in hospital the more likely you are to pick up some other illness. I've enough to contend with without that, thank you very much."

"I'll put the kettle on," Mrs Craemer offered, changing the subject before an argument ensued.

It was only an hour later when everyone left, but Chad

felt exhausted by the time they did.

"Come on, you need an hour on your bed," Fallon announced, much to Chad's annoyance.

"I'm not a baby in need of an afternoon nap," he snapped back at her, but was secretly glad to be given the opportunity to lie down. If he sat up much longer Chad was afraid he would make a fool of himself by fainting.

Fallon insisted on walking at the back of Chad as they made their way up the stairs.

"If I fall I'll take you with me," Chad argued.

"I'm here to make sure you don't fall," Fallon countered, one hand holding onto the stair rail and the other at the small of Chad's back.

"Bloody woman!" Chad chuntered. "You just love it that I can't fight back!"

"Too right," Fallon laughed, not unkindly. "How often does a woman get the opportunity to win a few battles against a man like you? You can be a real brute sometimes."

Biting back the sarcastic remark that was on the tip of his tongue, Chad silently admitted that Fallon was right. Not that he'd ever tell her so.

He actually didn't protest when Fallon turned down the sheets for him and helped him out of his clothes. Chad was exhausted and lifting his arms was more than he could easily manage.

"You really do look all in," Fallon told him when she sat on the bed after Chad had rolled into it.

He lay looking up at her, his eyes piercing in their intensity. "Thanks." It was all Chad said before falling into sleep, but it was enough for Fallon.

She sat for a long time staring down at the obstinate man she had been stupid enough to fall in love with. *I have no idea what the future holds for us, or even if there is an us, but I'm so glad you didn't die – I don't know what I would have done if you had died.*

Smoothing back his wayward hair, Fallon took full advantage of the fact that Chad was asleep to indulge herself. She drew her fingers through his hair and let it gently fall back into place. She touched a finger to his mouth, drawing it gently over the full bottom lip that she had loved to bite during their passionate kisses.

But they hadn't shared any of those intimate moments in the recent past, not since Chad had left her. *No, according to Chad he didn't leave me, just gave me the space I apparently asked for.*

But did you have to take off for so long?!

It had been hard on Fallon when Chad left, she didn't know if he'd gone for good or was just taking some time out of their relationship.

And she had missed him. Oh yes, Fallon had missed

Chad to the point of pain, a constant tearing at her heart that had sometimes felt like she would die of it.

Will you leave me again, Chad? When you're back on your feet and you get fed up on the farm, will you take off to some far off place to research and write your books?

It had been she who had wanted to travel before settling down to marriage, but now Chad was an author, able to work from anywhere.

It was tragic, really. They had split up because Chad was pressuring her into marriage and children and Fallon hadn't felt ready for either. Now she would give anything for Chad to give her another chance, but he hadn't asked her, hadn't even kissed her since his return.

Have I lost you forever, Chad? I hope not...with all my heart...I hope not.

CHAPTER SIX

It was only day 2 of Chad's stay with the Craemers and already he was chomping at the bit to get back to work on his latest novel.

"If you just get me my laptop I can work up here and you won't even know I'm around," Chad cajoled, restraining his temper just beneath the surface of annoyance.

"And that's exactly my point," Fallon replied, hands on hips her stance unrelenting. "You have a brain injury, so what do you want to do – you want to spend hours staring at a laptop screen taxing that brain until it hurts. No, I am not aiding you in giving yourself a massive headache – though why, I'm not sure, you've been giving me one for the past couple of days!"

He frowned like an angry grizzly bear at that. "Then maybe you should just let me move back home," Chad snapped back at her. "You're the one who insisted I stay here – I could have managed just fine back on my own farm!"

"Oh really," Fallon scoffed. "And we both know what you'd be doing right now if you were back home, so no, you're not going back there until I say so!"

Whether it was anger, or just her close proximity and the hell-fire of emotions she stirred in him, Chad couldn't tell, but he reached out and took Fallon's arm stopping her from slamming out of the room.

When she whirled on him, Fallon had been prepared to go another round with him, but Chad forestalled anymore arguments by covering her mouth with his.

At first, Fallon was too stunned to protest and then she was sinking into the kiss like a drowning woman. Too hungry to pass up such a delicious meal, Fallon feasted on Chad like she was afraid he would disappear again at any moment.

His hands were on her, remembering the feel of her body and wanting more. Chad's hands were not injured and worked diligently at undoing buttons and pushing aside her bra...when she groaned into his mouth it was almost Chad's undoing.

When he felt her nipples pebble against his palms, Chad knew he had to taste them and reluctantly broke the kiss to suckle at Fallon's breasts.

Her head fell back and her spine arched, Fallon couldn't give him enough of herself as his expert mouth drove her crazy with wanting and flooded her body with enormous pleasure.

This was what she had missed while Chad had been away, and had missed even more since his return.

Seeing him, watching him, knowing that Chad was only a short walk away from her had driven Fallon crazy. At least when he was gone she had been able to fall back on her anger to keep the love and the passion from eating her alive - but seeing him, day after day, and not being able to touch him, or be touched by him, had been nothing short of torture.

He'd undone the snap on Fallon's jeans and was gently tugging them down, following their progress closely with his mouth. Chad had another feast in mind and his mouth was eager to be on her, his tongue exploring her feminine folds and ultimately inside the moist heat of her sex.

Chad wanted the taste of his woman on his tongue, he'd gone too long without her to stop now. Anger had turned to urgent passion, Chad's wants and needs driving caution to the four winds and replacing it with a single-minded determination.

Only he was allowed to draw such moans of pleasure from this woman, and he revelled in his ability to do so.

Fallon was grinding her hips against him, begging his lips to move lower to ease the ache that was building inside of her and so deliciously centred between her shapely thighs.

Such was her eagerness, Fallon's hands moved from Chad's shoulders and her fingers dove into his thick thatch of hair. One moment she was on her way to heaven, the next she was in shock and filled with horror at the pain she had caused Chad.

His groan of agony had been more devastating than the sudden withdrawal of his hungry mouth.

"Oh God, Chad! I'm so sorry. I'm soooo sorry," Fallon cried in horror at seeing Chad's pale features and the pain written all over them.

Hurriedly tugging her jeans up, Fallon didn't bother fastening them or buttoning herself up again, her only concern was Chad and the pain he was in.

"Come on…" Fallon helped Chad to his feet and guided him over to sit on the bed "…let me look at the damage."

He grimaced as her fingers gently explored the site of

his wounds and was relieved when it was over.

"Jesus, Chad, I thought I'd opened up the wound or something – I was terrified of what I might find," Fallon admitted as she sat beside Chad on the bed.

"I suppose it's just a little tender yet for you to be clawing at my scalp the way you always used to," Chad chuckled ruefully. "But it was certainly worth a try," he grinned over at her.

Taking his hand and holding it between both of her own, Fallon had to choke back the tears that had suddenly sprung into her eyes.

"I've been thinking you didn't want me anymore, that maybe we were over for good this time," Fallon told him, her voice subdued and tremulous.

Letting out a heavy sigh, Chad slowly shook his head. "I've never stopped wanting you and I never will. When I tell a woman I love her, it isn't just so that I can get into her pants," Chad told her quietly, firmly.

"So...how many women have you said it to," Fallon smiled, though her insides were quaking as she waited for his answer.

He turned to look at her fully, taking in the nervous look in her eyes and the sad slope of her shoulders. "I've only ever told one woman that I love her, and I meant every word. It's just unfortunate that that woman didn't feel the same way – or not enough that she would marry me and want to bear my children.”

His voice had grown wistful, the longing not hidden as he watched Fallon's eyes turn away from him to look at their joined hands in her lap.

What should she tell him, that she would gladly bear his children right now if it would keep him at her side? After all, wasn't this what she had been praying for just a short while ago – to be given a second chance at happiness with Chad?

“It was never that cut and dried,” Fallon sighed. “I'm 24, I was 23 when you proposed and spouted on about having kids – is it so wrong for me to want a life of my own before I dedicate it, as I would surely want to, to our children?”

Watching her for a long moment, contemplating her words, Chad began to slowly nod his head. “Not the answer I wanted…” he frowned, pursing his sexy lips “…but understandable.”

She turned, then, her eyes out on stalks in amazement. “You mean it? You really understand?!”

Hell, it had been a blow to his pride when Fallon had refused his marriage proposal and told him she didn't want to have kids yet. But…

“I do now,” Chad qualified with a rueful smile. “I think

going off on my own for a while opened my eyes. I saw some harsh realities out there in the big bad world, it would be nice to be a little frivolous and enjoy some time on our own before we settle down to marriage and have to be grownups."

Fallon's mouth gaped open. "Who are you and what have you done with Chadwick Langdon?!"

He couldn't blame her for the dig, Chad had been stuck in his ways and difficult to budge when he'd set his mind to something. But being battered, almost to death, and almost losing everything and everyone he cared about, made a man take a fresh look at what was really important to him. And Chad surely had.

"You looked so sappy at Matt and Pam's wedding, I thought you had come round to the idea of love and marriage," Chad teased with a grin.

"I've never been against it, just not right now," Fallon told him. "Matt and Pam are different, marriage and kids has always been on the cards for them, they don't want anything more out of life than each other and the farm."

"But that wouldn't be enough for you...?" Chad asked, already knowing the answer.

"It isn't that I want fancy or expensive even," Fallon tried to explain. "But I do want to see more of the world than Dersley Dale before I pop my clogs off this mortal coil. We could travel in a camper van, stop off anywhere we wanted, take ferries to different parts of the world and see it all," she rambled excitedly, warming to the subject. "And you could write anywhere, get lots of research done and come up with some brilliant slasher crime novels-"

"I don't write slasher novels," Chad interrupted her on a laugh. "A few characters might get dead in some imaginative ways, but I definitely don't write slasher novels," he insisted.

Cocking a brow, her look said 'tell it to the hand', as she held one palm out to stop him. "I read your first novel, and I'm half way through the second – it's a good job I'm not squeamish, reading about all that arterial blood spurting from necks and covering walls and furniture!"

"Ok, they're a little bloody in places," Chad conceded, and Fallon rolled her eyes. "But the criminal underworld is like that – someone falls out of favour and the one in charge either takes care of the problem himself or orders an underling to do it for him. And I've seen for myself just how brutal the solutions to such problems can be," he nodded and cocked a brow tellingly.

"You got involved with these people...this criminal underworld," she gasped, terrified by the thought of Chad putting himself in such danger for the sake of a good story. "What the hell is wrong with you?! If someone hadn't tried doing it already, I might see if I could knock some sense into that thick skull of yours," Fallon ranted, getting off the bed to better vent her anger.

"You were never reckless as a kid – that was always Ashton's territory – but now…" she threw her hands up in the air as she paced in front of him. "Chad, it isn't just me, you have to think about your parents, your mother – how would she feel if you turned up dead like one of your fictional characters? Dead is dead, there's no rubbing it out and rewriting the scene," she told him angrily.

Taking his cue, Chad stood, pulling her to him and felt Fallon go stiff, still fuming at him. "First of all, I was never in any real danger," he lied. "The boss knew what I was doing and why I was there – he liked the idea of having his stories told in a book – made him feel famous, even though I used fictional names and places," Chad chuckled, remembering the conversation he'd had with Max Dolan.

'You use any of my boys' names, you're dead. You get in the way of my business, you're dead. You cost me money…I'll kill you myself and take my time about it…then you'll be dead!'

That wasn't a conversation he'd ever share with Fallon, not if he wanted to keep his head on his shoulders – she could be fierce when riled!

"So, what, you just walked into some mob boss's place and said 'I want to write a story about you'?" she asked sceptically. "And he, being ever so polite and obliging, just said 'yeah, sure, come sit with me kid and I'll tell you a few good ones to get you started,'" Fallon scowled up at Chad, sarcastic disbelief painted all over her pretty face.

He couldn't help the laughter that bubbled from him as he compared her image to the way it had really happened. "Max was alright, you just had to know how to read his moods. Then you had to learn when to stay still and when it was better to duck and run."

Her gasp was audible and made him laugh even harder. "Kidding! Just kidding," he lied again, and got a thump on his broad chest for the trouble.

Feigning injury, Chad pulled a pained face and groaned just enough to have Fallon look at him with anxious regret. "Oh god, I forgot – did I hurt you again?"

"It jolted my head a bit," he said, putting a brave smile on just for show. But when Fallon put her arms around him and kissed his chest, he couldn't find it in him to feel guilty about it.

"So, back to where we were earlier," his dark voice rumbled against her ear. "Pity we can't pick up where we left off, things were just starting to get interesting."

Unable to stop the tremor that ran through her at the

thought of just where they had left off before she'd ruined things, Fallon hugged Chad even tighter. "There's plenty of time for that, and I'll make it up to you when we are ready to indulge more freely."

"Hell, now you're getting me all stirred up again," Chad told her, pushing his erection into her soft flesh so that Fallon couldn't possibly mistake his meaning.

She drew back, her eyes twinkling with mischief and pleasure as they looked into his. "There's no point both of us suffering, and it was my fault things came to such an abrupt end…"

Leaving the words hanging in the air, Fallon dropped to her knees in front of Chad and made good on her promise to make it up to him.

CHAPTER SEVEN

"I bet Chad's giving Fallon hell," Matt laughed with Wesley and Pam in the stable yard.

"Don't be so sure..." Pam lifted a brow "...Fallon won't take any bull from Chad. She's more than capable of holding her own, whether it's against Chad or anyone else!"

Matt laughed and took a step away from her. "Hold on, I know you women like to stick together, but this is Chad we're talking about. No one gets one over on him, bashed in the head or not."

Wesley watched the newlyweds enjoying a bantering match, but stuck up for Pam on this one. "I'm afraid Pam's right – Chad won't get Fallon to knuckle under, she'd chew him up and spit him out before she'd let him get her under the thumb! My sister can be formidable when she wants her own way."

Shaking his head in wonder, Matt said, "Can't think how those two ever got together – not exactly a match made in heaven."

"Hell, more like," Wes chuckled.

But Pam just smiled and shook her head at them both. "You really don't get it do you – either of you?"

"Get what – that they're a pair of hard heads who'll spend the rest of their lives fighting if they stay together," Matt scoffed good humouredly.

"That's my point – neither one of them would be happy with a little mouse who gave in to their every demand – where's the challenge in that?!" Pam smiled.

"Challenge...? Sounds like a lot of head knocking if you ask me," Matt frowned. "I prefer a quiet life."

Pam smiled and gave him an under the lashes look that was sexy and shy at the same time.

Wes pushed off the wall he'd been leaning against and took the hint. "I'll see you two later – I promised Ashton we'd do something about now," he blustered, making his excuses before leaving them as quickly as his legs would carry him back up to the main house.

He bumped into Jackson and Lizzy in his haste, and Wes apologised for almost knocking the young girl over.

"It's alright..." Lizzy giggled as both men tried to stop her from falling to the ground "...I'm not as fragile as I'm thin looking."

"You're not thin..." Jackson protested "...just a bit slimmer than most. I think you've filled out quite nicely since you moved into the farm house."

Wes and Lizzy both looked at Jackson like he'd suddenly grown two heads. Then Wes turned to look at Lizzy and realised that Jackson was right.

"Actually, Jackson's right – I can see we're going to have to keep a closer eye on you Lizzy," Wes frowned as he took in her shapeliness. "You tell us if anyone starts bothering you – some lads, and men for that matter, don't know when to take no for an answer."

Lizzy's cheeks were burning by the time the two men had finished their open appraisal of her, and she could barely breathe for embarrassment.

"I'm sure I'll be just fine," she told them. "I've never had any trouble of that kind and I don't reckon It'll start now," Lizzy huffed. "Are we ready to go," she said pointedly to Jackson.

"I think we embarrassed the poor kid," Wes chuckled. "But I wasn't joking – our Lizzy is growing up and filling out in all the right places."

Jackson nodded. "Don't worry, we'll all keep an eye on

her. Our Lizzy is a bit too naive for her own good."

When Jackson pulled up outside of Lizzy's parent's house, he turned in his seat to look at the young girl.

"Lizzy, what Wes said back on the farm, you are careful when you go out, aren't you?" Jackson frowned with concern.

"Careful? You mean like Chad tells me about not going anywhere on my own?" she asked shyly.

"Well, that too – but I'm talking about boys…men, if someone makes you feel uncomfortable or bothers you in any way, you would tell us?" he asked, watching Lizzy closely.

She squirmed in her seat, just wishing to be gone. Her mother had given her 'the talk' the last time she was home and Lizzy had been mortified.

"I'll be careful," she assured him. "I'm not the sort to hang around with boys – I like my life on the farm, that's enough for me."

"That's good to hear," Jackson smiled and nodded. "We're just looking out for you, Lizzy. Take care," he told her as she climbed out the car. "I'll pick you up at 5pm."

Spending Friday with her family was just what Lizzy needed. She missed her little brothers and her mother was always glad of her help around the house.

"You're such a good girl, Lizzy," her mother said as

Lizzy dished up the boy's dinner. "They always look forward to seeing you – and so do I."

Her mother looked sad and Lizzy grew concerned. Knowing that her father could lash out when he'd had a drink or was tired from working nights, Lizzy wondered if he was hitting her mother again.

"Is everything alright with Dad?" Lizzy said once her brothers were settled at the dinner table. "He's not…"

She let the words hang in the air, not wanting to say 'hitting you' in front of the boys.

"I'm fine, Lizzy, and your dad seems to be a little better of late. I'm just a little tired myself," her mother continued, and Lizzy noticed the dark circles under her eyes and her pale cheeks.

"Have you seen the doctor, mum? Now I look, I can see that you don't look well," Lizzy frowned, narrowing her eyes to peer more closely at her mother.

"Don't fuss, Lizzy – I'll go to the doctor when I have the time. I have work this afternoon."

"Work!" Lizzy was aghast, her mother didn't look well enough to be going out to work. "Call them, tell them you're not well enough to come into work."

"If I don't work we don't eat," her mother declared firmly. Now stop fussing and quiet the boys down."

For the rest of the day Lizzy kept her brothers

occupied, taking them out to the local park for a couple of hours to wear them out.

By the time her mother came home, Lizzy would have them fed, bathed and changed into their pyjamas ready for bed.

It worried her to see her mother so unwell. Lizzy didn't know if it was serious or if her mother really was just tired, as she'd said.

Maybe I shouldn't be living at the farm – it's great for me but what about mum? Maybe dad's taking it out on her now that I'm not around?

I think I'll give Jackson a call and tell him not to pick me up tonight – I want to keep an eye on mum for a bit. And, anyway, if she is just tired, me putting the boys to bed and getting up with them in the morning will help.

"No, don't worry, Jackson, I'll be fine," Lizzy told him when he said he didn't like the idea. "It's just one night, and it'll help mum to get some rest. She needs it, Jackson, mum really doesn't look well."

Lizzy kept the boys in the breakfast room with her while her father watched television in the front room. Her mother went for a lie down on their bed for an hour...or two, and that was just what Lizzy had hoped for.

"Come on boys, let's do some puzzles together."

When her father came through the breakfast room,

on his way to the kitchen for another beer, Lizzy noticed the boys hunch down and bow their heads as if they were trying to disappear.

I remember how that feels, like you want to melt into the furniture so that dad doesn't see you. But I've never seen him hit the boys like he used to hit me – maybe it's only recently started?

"How would you like to go to the park for a little while," Lizzy asked them, and loved the way their little faces lit up as they nodded eagerly. "Alright then, let's get your coats and boots on."

Their father didn't even glance at them as they left the house, he was too busy watching football and drinking beer to notice them.

The boys skipped along in front of Lizzy and were obviously enjoying being out of the house.

It wasn't far to the park and they waved to a few of the neighbours as they went along.

"Hi, Mrs Brody…" Lizzy smiled at the neighbour who had always been so kind to her "…we're off to the park – let the boys run off some of their energy."

Mrs Brody chuckled. "They certainly are live wires – wish I could get a transfusion of some of their energy. Getting old is no fun, Lizzy."

"You're not old, Mrs Brody," Lizzy frowned in concern.

"Maybe you're just trying to do too much – do you need any help with anything? I could pop round in the morning if you do."

The woman was in her sixties – not old or frail by any means, but she was a house-proud woman and loved to keep her garden nice too.

"That's kind of you, Lizzy – but I'm just feeling a bit tired because I've had my grandchildren for a couple of days this week," Mrs Brody smiled. "They're about the same age as Lucas and Liam, and just as lively. But I do love to see them."

"Well, if you're sure," Lizzy waved and followed behind the excited boys as they began skipping to the park again.

It was actually quite a nice day – the sun was shining though it was still on the cold side, but it didn't seem to bother the boys.

"Hey, stay together so that I can keep an eye on you both," Lizzy warned. They giggled and headed for the slide, taking it in turns to ride it.

Lizzy had brought a ball with them and when the slide and the swings became 'boring' she got it out and joined them for a game of football, all the time unaware that they were being watched.

The men had been right, Lizzy was attracting

attention, only this time it could cost her, her life.

Another young family entered the park and their children played with the boys, allowing Lizzy to sit down for a while.

"Getting them to run off steam is the only way we get them to sleep at night," the young mother told Lizzy.

"I know what you mean..." she chuckled "...my little brothers can be quite a handful – I'm just getting them out of the house for a while so mum gets a break."

"I sometimes wish we had someone who could lighten the load a little, but we don't have any family living nearby," the woman confessed. "John moved here because of his job and I wanted a village home for the children. I didn't want them to grow up in a crowded city, so John commutes for work."

"It doesn't take that long using the motorway," her husband assured the young woman. "And I agree, village life will be much better for the kids, especially as they get older. City life can lead to trouble."

Lizzy knew about city life and trouble, a friend of hers had moved to Birmingham and had gotten into lots of trouble. His mother, Mrs Tennyson, had told her mother and it had gotten passed on to Lizzy. Apparently the police were involved and the Tennyson's were buying one of Matt's new houses so that they could move back to the village. Mrs Tennyson had said that moving to the city was the worst move they ever made.

"They look a bit older than my brothers..." Lizzy observed "...won't they start school soon?"

"Mia starts this September and Tyler will start next September," the young mother smiled. "And it's just like me to miss them terribly when they do start school – I don't really want them away from me, I just get a bit tired sometimes...that's all."

"I'd better get back with the boys..." Lizzy smiled as she stood up "...my mum will be wondering where we are."

"Your mum's very lucky to have a daughter like you. I hope Mia grows up to be just as caring." And the couple watched as Lizzy gathered her brothers together and told them it was time to go home.

"Bye." The boys waved goodbye to their new friends and then to their parents as they skipped past.

"I hope they sleep well for you tonight," Lizzy called out as she waved goodbye to the young couple, and then they were nearing the park gate so she turned to keep an eye on her brothers.

Unaware that they were being followed, Lizzy sang a nursery rhyme with the boys as they skipped all the way home.

So, your name is Lizzy and now I know where you live. I'll be watching you, Lizzy, then we'll get to know each other better. Much, much better!

<u>CHAPTER EIGHT</u>

Chad hated feeling weak and was determined to get out of the house today. But Chad also knew that he wasn't 100% yet, not even nearly, so when he went out for a walk by himself he didn't push it.

Christ, what a state to be in! If I ever meet the son-of-a-bitch who did this to me I won't just dent his skull I'll knock his flaming block off!

The weather seemed to be picking up a bit — it had been on the chilly side lately and the winds made it feel even colder than it was.

That's what weathermen call 'the wind chill factor', Chad smiled to himself. He didn't rate weathermen much, to his mind they got it wrong as often as they got it right so he deemed it scientific guess work.

He might have decided not to continue his life as a farmer, but Chad still had an appreciation of the land, of the beauty that surrounded him.

It's been a privilege to grow up here, to be welcomed back with open arms. I just wish Fallon could make up her damn mind what she really wants. Asking her to marry me wasn't just a whim on my part, I really see us having a good life together.

And one minute she doesn't want children then she's talking about how much she will want to dedicate herself to their care – what am I supposed to make of that! And they say men are hard to understand – we have nothing on the complexities of women!

Chad watched as Wesley walked towards him from the direction of Langdon Farm. They had traded places for a while on Fallon's insistence so that she could supervise Chad's recovery.

"Hey…" Wes called in greeting having spotted his friend, "…does my sister know you're out and about?"

Frowning deeply, Chad gave a growl of dissention then said, "She's not my bloody keeper – though she acts like it! I just needed to get out for a while, see some open spaces instead of looking at the same four walls."

"Understandable," Wes smiled agreeably. "I'm working on the tractor out in the fields today – you could ride along with me if you've a mind?"

"Got time for a walk before you start?" Chad asked, reluctant to go back inside yet.

Wes took the time to give Chad a look over before he agreed. "We'll head for the river, but you make sure and tell me when you've had enough, right?"

"Right," Chad smiled and nodded.

From the kitchen window, Fallon watched as the two most important men in her life walked off instead of coming in as she'd hoped.

"I hope Wes doesn't take Chad too far – he needs to be able to make it back again," Fallon worried, talking absently to her mother.

"Wes is more responsible that you give him credit for," Mrs Craemer told her. "It's about time Chad pushed himself a bit, you've kept him cooped up long enough."

"I'm just doing what's best for him," Fallon defended, bristling at her mother's gentle chiding. "If it were left to him he'd be sitting at his laptop writing from dawn till dusk – he wanted me to go fetch it for him the minute he arrived here!"

Giving a soft chuckle at her daughter's umbrage, Sheila Craemer gave Fallon's arm a consolatory pat.

"I suppose he'll want to move back home soon," Fallon sighed as she continued to watch the two men slowly walking away. "Chad's headaches seem to have eased, though he still loses his balance at times – usually when he gets up too quickly, I think."

"He's done well to come through such a serious injury as well as he has," Mrs Craemer observed as she took the kettle off the stove and filled it under the tap. "The man who did it to him still hasn't been caught, and that's a real worry to me. If he's the same one as murdered those poor women, then he was here in this village and, for all we know, still is."

"We're all being careful," Fallon smiled, rubbing her mother's arm in comfort. "And we're all big enough to take care of ourselves, you should stop worrying."

Sheila Craemer gave a huff of indignation. "Oh should I now – well I'll have you know it's a mother's job to worry, and it doesn't stop when her children have grown up. If anything I worry about you all more now than when you were kids – at least then you only got scraped knees and maybe the odd broken limb...but now..."

She was remembering how hurt Fallon had been when Chad had taken off so suddenly. *Hearts get broken and aren't easily mended – a mother can't kiss that kind of hurt better, much as she might want to.*

Jackson was working the cattle with his father today – they were moving them to a neighbouring grazing field where the grass was green and lush.

"Lizzy said she wants to stay over another night," Jackson told his dad as he opened the gate to allow the cattle through. "She's worried about her mam's health – I just hope it isn't anything serious."

"Hmm…" Mac grumbled worriedly "…I just hope that waster of a father doesn't start on her again. If he does, Chad will be round to see him whether he's well enough to or not!"

"You don't really think he'd hit her again, do you?" Jackson hadn't thought it likely so hadn't worried about it.

"When a man is a slave to drink, you don't know what he's capable of once he's had a few," Mac warned ominously.

They concentrated on getting the last of the cows through the gate then locked it behind them.

"I don't like the sound of that – Lizzy's come on a lot since she's lived here on the farm, but she's still just a little thing compared to a full grown man," Jackson frowned.

"Maybe you could give him a warning – remind him that we're all watching out for Lizzy, and what will happen if she ever comes home battered and bruised the way she did before," Mac observed, giving his son a nod of approval.

"I need to go into the village – maybe I'll call into the

pub at lunch time and see if he's in there," Jackson smiled dangerously.

Lizzy was busy with her little brothers, her mother in bed and feeling very lethargic.

"Come on now, mam is trying to get some rest," she told them when the boys screamed and giggled, chasing each other round the breakfast table.

When her father came in, Lizzy made a grab for the boys before he could swing out with the back of his hand to lash at them.

Her worst fears had begun to come true, now that she was out of his nasty reach their dad had started in on Lucas and Liam.

She'd noticed the bruises on them when she'd bathed them before bed the night before, but when Lizzy had asked about them both boys had gone very quiet.

Gathering them to her, Lizzy gave her dad a look that pleaded with him not to hurt them and he had snorted in disgust before leaving the room.

A few minutes later, Lizzy heard the front door slam shut and knew her father had gone out for his lunchtime pint. *Good! Though he'll be the worse for it when he gets back. Why can't he be like other dads and just love his kids? It's not like we've ever given him a minute's trouble.*

But when her dad returned from the pub he did no

more than give them a resentful frown and laid himself on the settee to sleep off the drink.

Lizzy didn't like that he hadn't snarled at them, didn't trust his mood not to turn violent in a blink, so she kept the boys well away from him and took them out to the park again.

"We like it when you're home, Lizzy."

The boys danced in front of her, skipping along with happy smiles pinned to their little faces.

"I miss you both when I'm away," she told them. "But it's where I work and I have to start very early in the morning, so it makes sense for me to live there."

But Lizzy was having doubts about her living arrangements – if their dad had starting taking his moods out on the boys then maybe she ought to move back in.

At least I'm big enough to stand the pastings – the boys will break under his fists. I bet he's only started it since mam's been ill – the coward wouldn't do it in front of her, he never has!

Taking great care to keep the boys occupied, Lizzy indulged them on the park for most of the afternoon, taking them to the small refreshments pavilion to buy them an ice cream and a glass of pop.

"Thanks Lizzy, it's been great."

The boys always talked as one – whether it was Lucas

who spoke or Liam, the words spoke for both of them and they always looked to each other for approval.

"I've really enjoyed it too," Lizzy grinned. "I don't get time to play on swings and slides anymore."

The boys looked at each other and frowned. "That isn't fair, you should come back home and we could all go to the park every day."

The simplicity of a child's world had never hit her as it did now. Her little brothers were starting to grow up, but play was still at the heart of their little universe.

"I'd still have to go to work even if I did come back home," she reminded them. "I have to earn my keep and I really like what I do."

But that pleasure had Lizzy feeling guilty. While she was working with the horses she loved, her brothers, and probably her mam, were being terrorised by her dad.

The boys ate their ice creams in a contemplative silence. *Heaven knows what they make of things, but I can't go on living at the farm if they're in harm's way!*

"Come on, slow coaches..." Lizzy rolled her eyes playfully at her brothers "...we won't have time to do any fishing if you don't hurry up."

The boys looked at each other then burst into the brightest of grins. "Fishing!" they said together.

"You stay here and finish your pop, I'm just going to

buy a couple of fishing nets from the lady," and Lizzy pointed to the woman who had served them earlier.

As she walked away, Lizzy heard the boys talking animatedly about who would catch the biggest fish. It broke her heart to think of them alone and scared while she was living the high life at the farm and knew she wouldn't be going back.

When she returned to the table both boys were waiting expectantly and Lizzy handed them each a fishing net. "I've got one too, we'll see who catches the most fish – I think it'll be me," she challenged playfully.

Just as she had hoped, the boys laughed and argued their own case, stating that boys were better than girls at fishing.

"Well, we'll just see about that," Lizzy warned, and lead the excited boys to the stream at the far end of the park.

It was a warm sunny day and the little family were totally oblivious to the evil hovering in nearby bushes.

He was almost slavering at the thought of her young body and what he wanted to do to it. But he would wait, no point spoiling the fun with two little runts in the way.

No, he would watch and wait – the build-up was almost as good as the deed, he'd come to realise. Once it was over he would have to move on, search out another beauty to enjoy — but for now, Lizzy was keeping him entertained.

His trousers grew uncomfortable; his pulse raced and his hands became clammy, his dark mind filled with images of all the other young women he had enjoyed then throttled as he'd climaxed inside them.

CHAPTER NINE

It was getting easier to go through the exercise routine that Chad had set himself. He made sure to do it when Fallon and her mother weren't around, he didn't need women fussing over him telling him that he was doing too much too soon.

I'm going to get my laptop if it's the last thing I do today, he told himself, groaning as he pushed to do one more sit-up. *Then I'm going to get down all these ideas that have been crowding my head and let lose all the pent up frustrations on a good murder scene. Yes, I'll just imagine I'm killing the bastard who broke my skull!*

He pushed himself to finish the exercises and felt better for doing so. Chad was beginning to rise to the challenges the injury had presented and was glad to be coming out the other side.

And I have an idea what to do about my other little problem – if Fallon won't listen to reason then I'll just have to force her hand. She's mine, and I don't give a damn about all her prevaricating. If she didn't love me, that would be another matter, but she does and she'll marry me before the year is out, damn it!

The walk to the Langdon farmhouse was a long one. As kids the Craemer's and the Langdon brood had run between the farmhouses like it was a five minute stroll in the park, but Chad was feeling his aching leg muscles by the time he walked through the front door.

"Hey, bro, what are you doing here?" Matt grinned as Chad made to walk past the open office door.

Taking a breath, Chad turned back and entered Matt's office to give him a smile. "I managed to escape for a while – I swear, the Craemer women are worse than mother hens – I've barely been out of sight of one or other of them!"

Chuckling deeply, Matt gave his older brother a smile of sympathy. "Take a load off and I'll get you a mug of coffee."

Taking the visitor's seat nearest the desk, Chad groaned as his legs bent and his muscles protested.

"You sure you're not doing too much too soon," Matt asked, looking somewhat concerned.

"Good christ, not you too!" Chad frowned on hearing the words both Fallon and her mother had cautioned him with every single day since he'd been there.

Putting the mug of black coffee on the desk in front of Chad, Matt retook his seat and grinned over his steaming mug of tea.

"I gather you're being fussed over?"

The frown deepened and Chad looked fierce. "You can say that again! How the hell am I supposed to get better if I don't actually do anything?! I was damn glad to see Wes the other day, I went along for the ride when he was working the farm on his tractor. Christ, I need a bloody holiday!"

That comment put an idea in Chad's head and when Wes walked into the house then the office, he decided to put the idea into action.

"Hey, should you be here?" Wes asked, and earned a fierce scowl from Chad for his trouble. Holding his hands up and out in surrender, Wes laughed and backed away. "Just asking – my sister can be a bit of a tyrant when she's playing doctors and nurses – I know from experience, believe me."

"Can you play doctors and nurses when you're brother and sister?" Matt asked with a mischievous grin.

"Not the kind you mean," Wes chuckled deeply. "But

when Fallon has her nursing head on you'd better do as she says or she'll find a way to hurt you!"

Chad listened and reluctantly allowed himself a smile. "Your sister is not the only one; your mother is a fuss-pot too. But they mean well."

Wes made himself a mug of coffee and pulled up a chair. "Getting you down, is it?"

Giving a shrug of his broad shoulders, Chad brushed it off. "It was good of Sheila to let me stay – they both have enough to do without spending time waiting on me."

"They love having someone to fuss over," Wes told him. "I'm just glad it's not me."

Chad nodded and looked thoughtful. "I was just telling Matt that I could do with a holiday...I was thinking of taking Fallon away with me to say thank you for the care she's been heaping on me."

His brows shot up and Wes sat back on his chair to study his friend. "Chad, don't get mad but, are you sure you're up to travelling – it hasn't been that long since you had your skull smashed in?"

"I'm not talking about right now," Chad blew out a frustrated breath. "I was thinking in a couple of weeks."

Matt and Wes exchanged a look and Chad put his empty mug down on the desk with a resounding thud. "You two are as bad as the women – I'm not a bloody invalid!"

"Chad, you gave us all a scare, the doctors weren't at all sure that you were going to pull through," Matt reminded him.

Pulling in a lung full of air, Chad let it out slowly and reigned his temper in. "I appreciate that, and I appreciate that everyone is just looking out for me-"

"But you'd rather we left you the hell alone," Wes broke in and grinned.

Pushing a hand back through his longer than usual hair, Chad felt the short bristly hair that was growing back over his injury. "I don't know how I feel, and that's the truth. One minute I'm as weak as a flaming kitten and the next I'm twitchy for something to do. I hate not being able to just do whatever it is that I want to do when I want to bloody well do it!"

Nodding his understanding, Wes reached out a large hand to pat his best friend's arm. "You're doing brilliantly, and maybe you're right about the holiday. As long as you don't decide on Australia, I doubt a short trip to a hot beach and some relaxation will do you any harm. Just give it another couple of weeks, or so."

It all happened in the blink of an eye, or so it seemed to Lizzy when she looked back on what had happened.

They'd run out of milk and the boys would need some for their breakfast in the morning.

They're fast asleep and mam said she'll keep an ear out for the boys in case they wake. She pulled on her coat, a nice warm one that Pam had given her, then Lizzy slipped her feet into shoes and set off for the village.

Her mother had been concerned about the lateness of the hour and warned Lizzy to hurry and not stop for anything.

But Lizzy had brushed her concerns away, saying that she was fast on her feet and would be back before she was even missed.

In the back of her mind Lizzy could hear Chad's warning words and knew he would be angry if he ever found out that she'd been out alone at 10 o'clock at night. *So I'd better be quick and make sure Chad doesn't find out. He may not be as scary as he used to be but I still don't want to get him mad at me.*

It was just a 10 minute walk to the off-licence and Lizzy did it at a run that took only 3. Once she'd stepped out of her front door, Lizzy had been more scared than she cared to admit, even to herself, and had probably set a new speed record.

Gripping the carrier bag with the precious milk inside it, Lizzy prepared to set another record in her dash for home.

Her eyes darted around, searching the shadows for

any sign of danger, then Lizzy sprinted forward and into the dark night.

She heard the groan and muttered apology of someone who had barrelled into someone else and the angry oath in reply.

"Get the fuck out of my way," someone shouted, pushing a drunken man away from him.

"I said I was sorry, didn't I?" The drunk protested, and Lizzy realised with a jolt that it was her father.

Then Lizzy saw the glint of a knife and realised that the stranger intended using it on her dad. All memories of him pounding his fists into her and the hateful words he spat at her while he did so, fled her mind as Lizzy sprang into action.

The man was going to kill her dad and she couldn't just stand by and watch it happen.

She flew in the direction of the struggle and heard her father cursing the stranger as he tried to battle him off. Then she was on the man's back, having leaped as she'd seen the glint of the knife again and her father's shocked eyes when he'd seen it too.

With no thought for her own safety, Lizzy clawed at the man's face, pushed a thumb into his eye and shouted blue murder for someone to help them.

The stranger dug his fingers into her thigh, trying to

drag her off his back, but Lizzy didn't feel a thing. Adrenaline was fuelling her attack and she wouldn't let go of the hold she had around his neck.

If she let go he would kill her, would kill her dad and then get away – she couldn't, wouldn't let that happen.

Her legs, grown stronger with all the horse-riding, were clamped around his body and she rode him and held on no matter what he tried. Then an idea struck her and she kicked out with one leg and brought the heel of her foot back sharply into the man's groin.

His howl of pain was loud as he fell to his knees, then Lizzy felt herself being dragged off his back as people seemed to appear from everywhere.

She fought the hands that tugged at her, not wanting the stranger to get away. "Get off me! Get off me!" she yelled, the arm around the man's neck almost cutting off his airway as she fought not to let go.

"Lizzy! Lizzy! It's alright, we've got you now."

She knew that voice and it began to sink in that the danger had passed. Allowing the big hands that were pulling at her back to ease her off the stranger, Lizzy turned her head to see Wesley smiling down at her then went into a dead faint.

CHAPTER TEN

When Lizzy awoke in her bed at the farmhouse, she saw three tall men looking down at her.

Matt gave her a warm grin. "There she is, our brave warrior is back in the land of the living."

Wes chuckled and lifted her tiny hand off the bed to hold it very gently in his much larger hand. "You gave me a fright, Lizzy – I thought the bastard had stuck you with that bloody knife when you fainted in my arms."

Smiling weakly, Lizzy said, "Sorry, I don't know why I fainted, never have before."

Chad stood on the other side of her bed and Lizzy turned worried eyes to look up at him when he snorted in disgust. "I should take you over my knee and paddle your backside until you can't sit down," he frowned deeply.

Hearing Matt and Wes give a muffled laugh, Chad frowned over at them. "Go on, encourage her why don't you – she only put herself in mortal danger, for god's sake!"

When the two men looked properly chastised, Lizzy felt guilty that it was because of her and made to tell Chad so. But before she could utter a word, Chad went into a tirade worse than she could have imagined.

His arms moved expressively as Chad paced the floor at her bedside, his language bluer than she'd ever heard it before. How could she be so stupid, hadn't he told her not to go out on her own, not to put herself at such risk – and all for a bloody pint of milk, he'd ranted, on and on and on.

When he finally stopped pacing and stood looking down at her, Chad felt like a heel when he saw Lizzy's bottom lip tremble.

"You can take on a murdering maniac yet a few angry words from me reduce you to tears," Chad frowned, then surprised everyone by pulling Lizzy up and into a firm hug. "If you ever do anything as stupid as that again I'll throttle you myself, you hear me?!"

Matt and Wes grinned at each other, but straightened their faces quickly when Chad stood himself up and frowned over at them.

Then a fraught silence hung in the air and Lizzy saw a look pass between the men that she didn't understand.

"What's wrong...?" she asked, looking up at Chad for some sort of explanation.

Pursing his lips, Chad lowered himself to her bed and sat looking at the young girl who had wormed her way into his heart. As gently as he could, Chad knew he had to tell her the dreadful news.

"Lizzy, you've proved yourself to be as brave and courageous as any man in this room," Chad told her, and Matt and Wes gave her a nod of confirmation. "But we need you to use that courage in a very different way." He sighed heavily, his eyes falling to look at the frail hand he held, then Chad steeled himself to get on with it.

"My dad's dead...isn't he?" Lizzy said, pre-empting Chad's struggle to find the right words.

"We're sorry, Lizzy..." Matt said, his smile sad now "...he was too far gone by the time the paramedics got to him."

"Oh God!" Her hands flew to cover her mouth as Lizzy let out a sob. "What will mam and the boys do now — I've let them down so badly."

"No!" Chad bit out, startling Lizzy. "You did more than most would have done in your place, and a lot more than your dad deserved. I won't have you blaming yourself —

are you listening to me Lizzy," he added when she just lay there shaking her head.

"He's still dead and the boys and mam will be so upset," Lizzy moaned out, tears slipping down the side of her face onto the pillow. Then her eyes went wide and she grabbed at Chad's hand. "Do they know…has anyone told them?"

Letting out a sigh, Chad recalled the conversation he'd had with Lizzy's mother and the poor woman's sobs as Pam had tried to comfort her.

"Why didn't you tell us that your mother was so ill," Chad asked, surprising Lizzy again.

"She's tired, worn out she says, that's why I stayed a bit longer so I could take care of the boys and let her rest," Lizzy explained.

"She isn't just tired, Lizzy," Chad informed her, his voice full of concern. "We called a doctor and he confirmed that she has pneumonia, a very severe case of it," Chad emphasised gently.

"Mam?" Lizzy looked confused, then alarmed as the meaning sank in. "Is she going to die? Is mam going to die?" she asked, frantic now.

"The doctor had her admitted to the hospital and Pam went with her," Chad explained. "Pam phoned earlier and said the doctors thought they had caught it in time, but it all depends how your mother responds to the treatment," he cautioned, not wanting to minimise the seriousness of her mother's condition.

Dragging herself into a sitting position, Lizzy pulled in her emotions and turned her mind to what needed to be done. "What about the boys – if mam's in hospital, where are Lucas and Liam?"

"We made up one of the spare rooms," Matt told her, then grinned. "They're a bundle of energy, I read them one of my old story books and they pretended to be pirates – that's what the story was about," Matt explained with a chuckle.

"So they're here, in bed asleep?" Lizzy asked, feeling somewhat dazed.

"You have nothing to worry about, Lizzy," Chad told her firmly. "Just rest up and let us take care of things for a while."

She looked at Chad then and wondered why she had ever been afraid of him. "You're such a kind man..." Lizzy told him, managing a small smile "...not at all scary really."

Chad huffed and shifted uncomfortably when he heard his brother and Wes chuckle. "I'm plenty scary when I'm riled," he told her. "And if you ever do such a fool thing again I'll show you just how scary I can be!"

But Lizzy's smile only grew as she finally saw through

his stern façade. "Well, I'll try my best not to make you mad, and I'll thank you again for all you're doing for my family."

Pushing up off the bed, Chad gave her a fierce frown and said, "You're welcome," then walked out of the room without a backward glance.

"You've embarrassed him," Matt chuckled, and Wes joined in with a nod. "I don't think I've ever seen Chad look so awkward – he's usually so in control."

"He's the eldest – he had to be," Lizzy told them knowledgably.

"Yes, you'd know about that," Wes agreed. "You've been taking on the weight of responsibility to help your mother – you should have told us what was going on, Lizzy. We could have helped."

"Sorry, I didn't think," Lizzy told them. "And now my mam is in the hospital and I don't know how I'll look after the boys and do my work as well – Pam will have to sack me, she'll have to get someone else in to do my work. I don't even know if we have enough money to bury my poor dad," Lizzy finished on a sniff, her bottom lip beginning to tremble again.

"No one is going to sack you," Matt told her firmly. "As for the boys, we'll get them helping out in the stables to keep them occupied. We'll all help keep an eye on them – a farms a pretty neat place for kids, if they're watched properly."

"They're good boys," Lizzy smiled. "Full of energy and questions, but there's no harm in them."

"Not like us then," Wes grinned at Matt. "When we were kids we got into all kinds of trouble – Chad included," he added, and got a disbelieving smile in return.

"Oh yes, my brother was no saint," Matt backed his friend up. "He might be a bit stiff necked now he's older, but he was in trouble as much as we were when we were kids."

That wasn't quite true, but Lizzy seemed to be enjoying the thought of it and they embellished a few stories to take her mind off her troubles.

Downstairs, Chad was looking into the arrangements for her father's funeral. *Can't think he's left enough money for his own burial – would have drunk it all away if I'm any judge.*

It was getting late and he called the hospital to get an update on Lizzy's mum only to be told that they were not allowed to give any information out over the telephone. So he'd had to wait for Pam to get back to know how bad the situation really was.

He thought of Lizzy, of the way she had waded in when her father was being attacked, and felt a chill run down his spine.

Bloody fool could have gotten herself killed, why don't people listen when they're told not to go out by themselves, damn it!

It struck him then, if it hadn't been for Lizzy's father drunkenly walking into the man and causing the fight that got him killed, the murderer might have taken Lizzy and she could have been added to his list of victims.

Christ, what a thought!

He thought of Fallon, too — she had been royally pissed when he'd called to tell her where he was so that she and her mother wouldn't worry about him.

"You walked over there?!" she had demanded hotly. "Are you crazy, or did that maniac knock a few screws lose in that thick head of yours!"

Oh yes, his woman had been full of hell's fire and spitting blasts of it down the phone at him. *And I've never wanted her more! She's a handful, alright, but I wouldn't have her any other way.*

When he went to bed, just before midnight, Chad thought of Fallon and smiled. He lay back on his pillows staring up at the ceiling as the moonlight flickered over it.

I'm going to whisk you away, my lovely hell-cat, and I won't bring you back until we're married.

He fell into sleep with the smile still on his lips and dreamed of Fallon and the many ways he wanted to love her.

CHAPTER ELEVEN

"Why the hell I bother with the man, I have no flaming idea," Fallon fumed to her mother in the farmhouse kitchen. "He's an ingrate, a stubborn bull of a man with a huge dollop of arrogance thrown in!"

But he's mine, and for all his shit, I wouldn't have it any other way. When I thought I was going to lose him…

Fallon shuddered, she wouldn't think about that. Couldn't think about it or she'd lose the mad she'd worked up and wouldn't be able to give him what for when he walked back through their front door.

And she planned to give him a good talking to, had rehearsed it in her mind over and over again. Why hadn't he at least asked her to accompany him if he wanted to go over to his family's house, at least that way she'd have been there to help him if he'd tired too much along the way.

But no, he had to go off all by himself, as stubborn as a bloody mule and just as thick headed!

When the doorbell rang and she went to answer it, Fallon felt the steam coming out of her ears. *Now we'll see what's what!*

He stood there, this bull of a man she loved, looking all but done in and trying desperately not to show it. His spine was straight, his chest puffed out, but she could see the hurt in his eyes.

For one minutia of a second, Fallon thought about the tirade she'd had planned for him and then her temper dissipated and was replaced by nothing but love.

She didn't fuss over him, new that Chad was trying to regain some of the pride and stature he had lost due to his unfortunate injury. So she stood back, let him walk past her into the kitchen with his precious laptop tucked under his arm.

"Sit down the pair of you…" Sheila Craemer told them kindly "…the kettles just boiled so I'll make us all a nice cup of tea."

"You ok?" Fallon asked quietly, and watched as Chad nodded gingerly. He had a headache, she knew, could see it in his eyes, but decided not to say anything.

"Not too bad…considering," Chad smiled ruefully. "What with Lizzy and her crazy stunt when she took on that bloody murdering bastard," Chad said without thinking then smiled an apology up at Sheila as she placed a mug of tea in front of him.

"I think that's the least he can expect to be called!" Sheila told him, surprising the young couple with her fierceness. "And well done Lizzy, I say – she was only trying to protect her dad, but she did us all a great service by catching that murdering bastard!"

Fallon didn't think she'd ever heard her mother swear and sat back to grin at her.

"I say it as I see it…" Sheila lifted her chin "…and that man doesn't deserve civilities. I hope they lock him up and throw away the key!"

"Here, here," Chad agreed, holding up his mug of tea in salute, then the two women did the same. "To Lizzy," he grinned, and heard it repeated.

"It's a shame about her dad – I know he wasn't a kind man but he didn't deserve to die like that," Sheila said with compassion.

Fallon and Chad exchanged a look that said it all – as far as they were concerned he'd gotten exactly what he deserved.

"Her mother had to be taken into hospital," Chad

informed them, and both women gasped in shock. "Nothing to do with anything that happened," he reassured them. "I didn't know, when I called you last night, that Lizzy's mum has been ill for some time."

He shook his head in wonder. "Why Lizzy didn't tell us about it I just don't know. I think her mother managed to convince her, and probably herself, that she was just worn out and needed rest. Can't imagine that man gave her much of it when he was alive," Chad murmured.

"And...?" Fallon said when Chad fell silent.

"Oh...yes...she has pneumonia – I called a doctor after I went to tell her about what had happened," he explained. "She could barely stand to answer the door – I felt guilty as hell that I'd dragged her out of bed."

"Sounds to me like you did her a great favour by doing so," Sheila told him, patting the back of his hand on the table. "Is she in a bad way then?"

"I'm afraid she is," Chad confirmed grimly. "I've tried to play it down with Lizzy – not lying to her exactly, just not clueing her in on everything the doctors told Pam."

"It's life threatening," Fallon said succinctly, and watched Chad nod sorrowfully.

"I hate to think of Lizzy having to cope with the loss of both her parents, but there is a possibility that could happen," Chad confirmed.

"She has two little brothers, doesn't she?" Sheila asked.

"She does. If the worst does happen, and I'm praying it doesn't, then we'll need to help Lizzy get custody of them and bring them to live on the farm," Chad told them, a frown creasing his handsome brow.

"And you'd do that, take on that kind of responsibility?" Fallon asked, amazed and in awe of his generous spirit.

"Of course," Chad said without hesitation. "Lizzy would be devastated if they were taken into care."

Fallon smiled – he might use Lizzy as an excuse, and maybe that was genuine, but Chad would be upset if he allowed two such young boys to be taken into care, and she knew it.

"They'd have plenty of carers to look after them," Sheila said contemplatively. "Jackson and Mac both have experience of watching young children grow up on a farm, and Matt and Pam will be on hand too."

"Exactly," Chad nodded in agreement, then paled when the pain in his head shot down the back of his neck at the same time as it speared into both eyes.

Sheila discreetly gathered their empty mugs and took them to the sink while her daughter tended to Chad.

"Why don't you take that laptop upstairs, I'll be up in a minute," Fallon told him.

"I think I will," Chad smiled gratefully, then thanked Sheila for the tea and left them to it.

The headaches came less often now, but the stress of the previous night had probably taken its toll. Chad sat on the edge of his bed, laptop resting on his knees, just glad to get a few moments alone.

I suppose I should be grateful if a few headaches is all I'm left with after what that maniac did to me. Chad pressed a hand to his painful eyes, then moved it to rub the back of his neck.

"Here, let me take that," Fallon said as she put down the milk and pain tablets she'd brought him to lift the laptop from his knee. "Take these and have a rest on the bed for a while...and no arguing," she warned when Chad raised his eyes to look at her.

But he didn't intend to. Instead he took the pills without protest, thanked her then rolled back onto the bed and closed his eyes.

He felt her take off his shoes and lay a blanket over him. "Fallon...I love you." It was the last thing he said before falling into the blessed relief of sleep.

She carefully sat on the bed and watched him sleep, her man was suffering and it didn't sit well. Reaching forward she stroked back his hair and said, "I love you, too."

In fact, Chad slept for 3 hours and felt much better for it. Opening his laptop, he went to work on writing the idea he'd had for his next book.

When Fallon found him still bent over his laptop an hour later, she was surprised to see him looking so well.

"That rest seems to have done you good," she smiled as she crossed the room to him.

"I don't like giving in to it, but you were right," he acknowledged, turning his chair to face her.

Raising her brows in mock shock, Fallon said, "Why Mr Langdon, I do believe that's the first time you've ever uttered those particular words."

Taking her hand, Chad pulled her onto his lap and buried his nose in her hair. "You are too big for your boots as it is..." he remonstrated playfully "...but when you're right, you're right – I'm just glad the headache's gone."

"It was a bad one," she stated rather than asked.

"Yes, one of the worst I've had," Chad admitted, then looked into her eyes with great concern. "There's no saying they won't get worse – the doctors did warn me they could," he told her. "That and the possibility of violent mood swings – though I can't say I've noticed any."

"No..." she smiled mischievously "...you've just been you're usual surly self."

He moved quickly, tickling her ribs in punishment. "Is that so," he jibed as she laughed and wriggled in vain, trying to get away from him. "I may have to get my own back for that wicked remark!" Chad moved his hands from her sides to hold her still then took her mouth with his.

The kiss was playful to begin with, but soon moved into the realms of longing, of need, of mate seeking mate.

This is what he had missed, had feared he had lost forever. His woman, all spitting hell-fire and stubborn as a bloody mule – Fallon Craemer, soon to be Fallon Langdon if he had his way, and Chad was determined he would, was the force that had kept his heart beating when he should have died.

The doctors had been very honest, were bemused by his survival and his quick recovery. They had thought it most unlikely that he would survive at all, let alone regain all of his faculties and functions to near what they had been prior to the head injury.

Now, as his hands cupped his woman's breast and he heard the thrill of it in her moans, Chad rejoiced in his second chance at life and took pleasure in the woman he held in his arms.

Her blood was racing, she could hear the rush of it in her ears, could feel the heat of it flooding her body. Fallon couldn't have helped herself even if she'd had a mind to protest, but protesting hadn't even entered her lovely head.

When his hand worked its way down her body, Fallon's knees parted in anticipation. She was already hot, already wet, and welcomed his expert fingers when they drove into her.

"Oh god, Chad."

He worked her hard, felt the wet warmth of her spill over his fingers as she came. "I want you, Fallon. I need you right now."

She stood momentarily, pushed her panties the rest of the way off. Reaching down, Fallon smiled salaciously as her eyes fixed on the rigid bulge in his trousers and her fingers slowly drew down the zip that was restraining it.

When his erection was freed it stood to attention and Fallon's eyes widened appreciatively. A bead of pre-cum gleamed temptingly and Fallon dropped to her knees then reached out a single finger to smooth it over the bulbous tip while she looked up and into Chad's rapt eyes.

"Jesus!" he gasped, then struggled to breathe when she took him into her mouth and worked him just as hard as he had worked her just moments before.

Their eyes remained locked, the vision of Fallon greedily feeding on his rock hard cock sent Chad's blood pressure into the stratosphere.

They may have different opinions about marriage and children, but in the bedroom they were fully in accord.

Fallon had always responded to his touch, and Chad had always known it. They were a match in every way — he just had to make her see that.

For now it was Fallon in control. She could see the delicious torment written all over his devilish face, the strain of holding himself back causing the pulse in his neck to stand out as it beat wildly.

Yes, I know what you want, know how to give you the exquisite pain of denied release but, in the end, the pleasure will be so much more!

Only when Fallon felt his thighs stiffen, his muscles bunch, and heard a guttural groan roll out between his parted lips, did she relent and draw her mouth away.

Chad groaned again, his control tenuous as he watched Fallon remove the rest of her clothes.

"Fallon," Chad said her name reverently. "You're so beautiful...so damned sexy...I need to be inside you," he told her as Fallon stood, fondling her own breasts, just out of reach.

With a sexy chuckle, Fallon moved closer, straddled his lap and took Chad's throbbing length in as deeply as her lithe body would allow.

For one blissful moment she sat still, the first thrill of

pleasure rocketing through her, and then she moved and the pleasure grew with every slip and slide of his penetrating erection.

He fed on her breasts, teeth scraping over the sensitive tips while his hands clasped her buttocks, kneading the firm round flesh and pulling her onto him so that Fallon was filled to the depths of her being with his painfully hard manhood.

Her breathing grew shallow and rapid, her eyes closing as the first ripple of pleasure began spreading out from her centre. And then Fallon imploded, her body shattering around Chad as he drove into her again and again.

She had thought him on the edge, couldn't understand when he continued to work her, moving her bottom so that he speared into her with thrusts that were rapid and deep.

Fallon hadn't had time to come all the way down before she felt her body tensing, readying to explode a second time.

"I can't," she breathed, her breasts heaving as she dragged in air. "Chad…"

But he was determined that she could, would rise to the dizzy heights of a second climax, and then he would go over with her.

"Feel me," he growled. "Take me in — all of me," he demanded hotly, covering her mouth with his to swallow Fallon's screams of excruciating pleasure as it ripped through her body and left her trembling in Chad's arms.

CHAPTER TWELVE

The funeral of Lizzy's father was delayed to allow her mother to recover from the pneumonia that had seen her hospitalised.

Two weeks after her father's death, Lizzy her mother, Lucas and Liam, stood at the graveside as his body was lowered into the ground.

Only her mother cried, Lizzy felt frozen, as if the reality of the situation hadn't yet hit her. She held on to the small hands of her brothers and listened to her mother's sobs.

How can she be so upset – he only ever gave her misery and pain? Did she really love such a hateful man, will she mourn him and miss him forever?

They listened to the words the preacher spoke but

didn't take a one of them in. It was the sound of his soft mellow voice that comforted rather than any consoling or religious meaning he tried to impart.

With Avis Langdon offering support, her mother thanked him as she turned from her husband's grave and walked back to the car that had brought them.

It hadn't been a lavish funeral and her mother hadn't wanted to serve refreshments back at the house, so when they walked away it was over, nothing more to dread or prolong the awful event.

All of the Langdon clan were in attendance and Charley Langdon offered his condolences as he watched his wife assist the grieving widow, then moved off to follow.

Pam was talking to her mother and Avis as Chad approached Lizzy. "Are you alright, Lizzy?" he asked kindly.

She still had hold of the twin's hands so was mindful of what she said in reply. "I'm fine. I need to help mam a bit when we get home, then I'll make my way back to the farm."

Putting a hand to her arm, Chad shook his head. "There's no rush, stay with your mother a while if that's what you want — I'll make sure you get paid."

When her bottom lip trembled and her eyes filled,

Lizzy looked up at Chad with eyes full of gratitude and hero worship. "You've been more than kind already, paying for all of this. I'll settle the boys and make sure mam is alright, then I'll come back to the farm."

He nodded, seeing the determination on her lovely young face. "As you like, Lizzy. But if you change your mind, just give us a call so we won't worry where you are, ok?"

Unable to speak, Lizzy nodded and turned away to follow her mother into the car that waited for them.

"She's really sad," Matt said at his brother's side. "I wish there was more we could do."

"I'm sure there will be, in time," Chad told him. "For now, we'll have to keep an eye on Lizzy, be there for her when she needs to talk and grieve."

"Looking at her now, it's hard to believe our Lizzy actually brought that murdering bastard down," Matt said, the amazement clear in his voice.

"There's certainly more to Lizzy than meets the eye," Chad smiled. "She has a lot of guts - I think that's what will get her through all of this."

In time, the farm settled back into its usual routine, though Chad still hadn't moved back home.

"Want some more bacon?" Sheila Craemer smiled over at Chad, happy to see his appetite fully returned.

He grinned like a mischievous boy and nodded.

"You're filling out again – I didn't like to see you looking so thin," Sheila told him as she heaped grilled bacon onto his plate.

"If I don't watch out I'll end up as fat as your prize pig," Chad smiled in thanks.

"I doubt it – those exercises you do no doubt burn off the excess," she told him, and moved to put the kettle on.

He was surprised, he hadn't known that Sheila was aware of the rigorous routine he put himself through daily. "I hope I haven't disturbed you," Chad said warily. "Does Fallon know?"

Sheila turned from the stove to regard Chad, then smiled and shook her head. "I know she's been fussing over you – would have hit the roof if she'd known what you were up to – but I decided you would know your limits and listen to your own body if it started to protest."

"Thanks."

Chad waited for Sheila to bring them both a cup of tea and sit herself down at the breakfast table, then he said, "At first, I did it just to feel normal, to prove to myself that I wasn't an invalid."

"Yes, I thought that might be it," Sheila smiled.

"But then I noticed the other effects – my mood was lifted the more I could do and the physical improvements were encouraging," Chad explained. "Not just my fitness..." he continued "...but my independence – and that was really important to me."

"I understand," Sheila nodded. "Being able to get out of the house must have been a big step and an empowering one."

"I was going stir-crazy," Chad chuckled, then realised what he'd said. "Not that I'm not grateful," he backtracked hastily. "You and Fallon have been brilliant, the way you put up with my moodiness and fatigue."

"We were all worried about you, Chad," Sheila told him seriously. "What that man did to you almost cost you your life and we're just grateful that it didn't – Fallon most of all," she added, her smile returning.

He looked at the woman who had been like a second mother to him and considered telling her everything. Her daughter was driving him insane and he might be able to enlist her mother's help in taming her.

Taking a sip of his tea, Chad looked over his mug at Sheila and smiled as he replaced it on the table.

"Sheila, your daughter is a strong willed woman with a fiery temper, but I love her more than life," he began, and grinned when she nodded in agreement. "That being the case, I have a plan to bring her around, but I'd need your help to pull it off."

Fallon had spent the night at Fenella's house – with her father still away trying to save his newspaper business and her mother staying with her sister, Fenella would have been left virtually on her own.

"I don't usually mind my own company…" Fenella told Fallon as she served her tea and biscuits in the lounge "…but with all that weird murder stuff going on, the house seems too big and scary to rattle around in on my own, but for the housekeeping staff."

"Can't say I blame you – thanks." Fallon took the cup and saucer that Fenella held out to her along with a couple of chocolate chip biscuits. "The fact that he was so close is what gives me the willies."

Taking a seat on a nearby sofa, Fenella shuddered. "I like to think I'd have been as brave as Lizzy, but I'm not so sure I would. I'd have been terrified and probably just run for help."

"That would have been the sensible thing to do," Fallon stated unequivocally. "It was sheer luck that Lizzy survived – her father was a big man and he didn't!"

Fenella's gaze fell to study her cup of tea, as if it held some mystic power of foretelling.

"Want to talk about it?" Fallon asked instinctively.

Frowning into her tea, Fenella eventually lifted her eyes to look at Fallon. "I suppose it's just the talk about fathers – I'm beginning to wonder if I'll ever see mine again."

Surprised by the observation, if not the focus of it, Fallon did her best to be tactful and supportive. "That's nonsense – nothing you've heard so far has indicated that he's going to be arrested."

Hesitating only momentarily, Fenella said, "I looked through his office, read some of his emails." She bit her bottom lip then continued quickly. "They were awful – I never would have believed my father capable of what I found, but...but it all makes a sick kind of sense," she broke off on a sob.

Getting to her feet, Fallon moved to sit by her friend and took her hand. "Nothing your father has done is your fault. No, it isn't," Fallon insisted when Fenella looked uncertain. "But if you keep quiet about what you found, if you bury your head in the sand, you will be complicit to anything he does from this moment on."

"I don't know what to do," Fenella sobbed, taking the tissue that Fallon held out to her. "It isn't as straight forward as you seem to think, yet I know you're right."

Frowning, Fallon considered then said, "Is your mother involved?"

Shocked that Fenella didn't immediately deny it, Fallon only squeezed her friend's hand and waited.

Heaving a sigh, Fenella shrugged. "I honestly don't know…though I doubt mother knows the extent of daddy's underhanded dealings." Steeling herself, Fenella prepared for her friend's horror and revulsion as she revealed the worst of her findings. "There are photos…in the bottom drawer of his desk, the one he always keeps locked…they're extremely graphic."

"Sex photos?" Fallon asked, thinking Fenella had discovered her father's pornography stash.

"Some," Fenella confirmed. "Politicians in compromising situations – I think my father used them for blackmail," she guessed, her voice barely audible. "But the others are worse…they're…they're…"

Fallon held her when Fenella burst into great big sobs that shook her from head to toe.

For long moments the two girls clung to each other and rocked on the settee. Then Fenella lifted her head and choked back the tears.

"I think my father may have had some people killed," Fenella blinked rapidly, dislodging more tears.

Shocked beyond belief, Fallon sat back to regard her friend steadily. "If you believe this, if you have photos to prove it, you have to give them to the police. You have to," Fallon insisted.

"I know that's what I should do," Fenella shot out as

she got hurriedly to her feet. "But my life would be over if I did. You know how it's been for me since all the rumours started about my father – no one in the village spoke to me or my mother, we were virtually ostracised!"

Yes, Fallon knew how bad things had been, hadn't she been just as judgemental as everyone else to start with? But to keep this kind of information secret – no, she couldn't let that happen.

"You realise that I'm involved now," Fallon said, staying seated and watching her friend as she wrung her hands. "I will be just as complicit if I say nothing of what you've told me. Can you really ask me to do that?"

The breath went out of her as Fenella sagged back down onto the settee. Her eyes closed and Fenella rubbed trembling hands over her face then looked at Fallon and shook her head.

"No, I know what I have to do, I just didn't want to face it." Her sigh was soul deep and Fallon truly felt for her. "I'll lose everything – everyone – even Jackson."

"Jackson?!" Fallon's shock was plainly evident.

"Yes," Fenella smiled shyly, sadly. "We've been seeing each other for a while now."

"You and Jackson – well you kept that one quiet," Fallon chuckled, somewhat bemused.

"We both thought it best, until we knew where it was

going," Fenella shrugged. "Now it won't matter – he won't want to see me after this all comes out."

But Fallon wasn't so sure. "I think you're grossly underestimating Jackson. He isn't the sort to be put off by something your father did – but if you keep it to yourself, if you hide those photos and say nothing..."

"You really think he'd be able to overlook the fact that my father may have had people killed?" Fenella asked, already shaking her head in disbelief.

"Why don't we ask him?"

"What?!"

Fenella was shocked and suddenly terrified of what Fallon was suggesting.

"You can't go to the police alone, it would be too much for anyone," Fallon stated matter of fact. "Ask Jackson to go with you – tell him what you plan to do and ask for his help. I think you'll be surprised by his answer."

"He'll probably run for the hills," Fenella replied, but the idea was a tempting one.

"Not a chance – Jackson has more spine than that. Call him – ask him to come over and sort it out right now," Fallon urged before Fenella could over think it.

"I...I..." Fenella struggled to breathe, to think, but then she put her hand into her pocket and pulled out her mobile phone. She stared at it for a long moment then up at Fallon who gave her an encouraging smile. "Alright, I'll do it, but you have to stay with me while I tell him."

"I'm not going anywhere," Fallon assured her.

The call was difficult but Fenella hadn't had to plead for long before Jackson agreed to come over.

"He's worried. I couldn't tell him anything on the phone, but he could tell I was upset," Fenella said as she stuffed her mobile back in her jeans pocket.

In less than five minutes, Jackson was at the door and knocking it rapidly. "Fenella. Fenella, what's going on?"

When Fallon opened the front door to him, Jackson took a step back in surprise. "Fenella is in the sitting room – please, just listen to her and be kind – she thinks you'll dump her once she's told you what she needs to."

Not saying a word, Jackson followed Fallon into the sitting room and strode over to where Fenella still sat on the settee.

"What's going on – why have you been crying?" Jackson asked, his deep voice full of concern.

"Do you need me to stay?" Fallon asked, still standing in the doorway.

Fenella looked into Jackson's eyes then back at Fallon. "Perhaps you could wait in the kitchen…just in case."

Closing the door, Fallon left them to discuss the information Fenella had found and whether or not they still had a relationship.

CHAPTER THIRTEEN

It was every bit as hard as Fenella had expected to tell Jackson the truth about her father, the only bit she got wrong was Jackson's reaction to it.

"God almighty, you must be devastated," Jackson stated, his blue eyes full of sorrow for this brave woman.

"It will get worse, all the shunning, the name calling and the gossip, it will all get worse once the police are informed," Fenella said, sucking in her bottom lip nervously.

"Not if I have anything to do with it," Jackson stated firmly. "If anything, the people of Dersley Dale, and beyond, should be admiring your courage – any that don't see it that way will have me to answer to if they speak of it in my hearing," Jackson assured her.

Flinging her arms around his neck, Fenella held on tight to the one person who seemed to see her for who she was and not just as the daughter of a crooked newspaper tycoon.

He held her, just wrapped his strong arms around Fenella and willed all his strength into her.

"I have to go to the police…" Fenella mumbled into his shoulder "…but I don't think I can do it on my own."

Pulling back just enough to look into her eyes, Jackson smiled. "You're not on your own, I'm right here."

"You're not going to dump me?" Fenella asked, still not able to believe her good fortune.

"Is that really the kind of man you think I am – that I would run at the first sign of trouble?" he asked, not taking his eyes from Fenella's.

She couldn't speak, but shook her head and closed the gap between them. Fenella poured her heart and soul into the kiss, into him, the only man who had ever truly cared about her.

"We'd better tell Fallon the coast is clear," Jackson chuckled softly when they finally drew apart. "I'll bet she's pacing the kitchen floor."

"And listening for the front door to slam behind you – I was so convinced you wouldn't want to stay with me after you knew the truth," Fenella smiled shyly.

"Hmm, well, I'll overlook your poor judgement of me in the circumstances," Jackson told her as he stood then held a hand out to help Fenella to her feet.

They crossed the sitting room together, arms locked around each other's waist and went to tell Fallon the good news.

Turning at the kitchen door, Fallon beamed as she watched the happy couple walk towards her. "I told you it would be ok," she stated with a look at Jackson and back to Fenella. "Are you going to the police now?"

Looking up at Jackson, Fenella nodded. "Jackson is going to come with me – I'm too much the coward to go on my own."

Before Fallon could reply Jackson said, "You're not a coward, I don't want to hear you putting yourself down like that – understand?"

Feeling his arm tighten about her waist, Fenella looked up and nodded.

This was a side of Fenella that Fallon had never seen – gone was the frivolous fashion plate, the tantrum throwing barbie doll to be replaced by this acquiescent young lady who was so obviously in love.

"If you want to go now, I can make your excuses at the farm," Fallon told Jackson, worried that Fenella might balk if given the time to do so.

"That's good of you," Jackson smiled. "We'd better gather everything up and take it with us," he said, looking down at Fenella.

To Fallon's surprise, Fenella's voice was strong and determined when she said, "Yes, there's a lot of it so we may need a box – I'd rather take it all in one trip."

Suddenly anxious that her friend fully understand the possible impact of her actions, Fallon found herself cautioning Fenella. "Fenella, this isn't just a case of dropping off what you've found – the police will want to search this house, will no doubt get some kind of search warrant that entitles them to take away your father's computer and anything else they think pertinent. It won't be a very nice experience," Fallon finished, touching her friend's arm gently.

Looking up at Jackson, Fenella smiled then turned to look back at Fallon. "I won't be facing it all on my own – Jackson will help me through it."

"Then I won't hold you up – I need to get back and see what Chad's up to," Fallon chuckled, then left them to do the awful deed.

For once, Chad was where Fallon had left him that morning but for some reason he looked relaxed and happy about it.

"I thought you might have made your way over to

your place," Fallon observed, taking a seat in the rarely used sitting room and watching Chad with suspicious eyes. "I just called in to tell them Jackson won't be back for a while – probably the rest of the day, actually."

Chad frowned curiously, "Why is that?"

"Because he's taken Fenella – who is totally in love with him, by the way – to the police station with a mountain of evidence against her father," Fallon explained succinctly.

"Well, well…so the mighty will fall because one of his own has turned on him," Chad smiled and nodded with some satisfaction. "I've wondered how much his family knew about his criminal activities."

For some reason, Fallon felt irked by his smug satisfaction at her friend's dilemma. "Fenella knew nothing about her father's 'criminal activities'," she spat out angrily. "That poor girl found out because she unearthed documents and photographs that pushed the truth of it in her face."

Fallon got up, she couldn't sit when her blood was racing around her body as the temper rose in her. "You men do just as you please and the women in your lives have to follow on meekly in your wake. Well don't expect me to be one of them, Chadwick Langdon!"

He didn't know how the conversation had gone from

Theodore Swain's criminal activities and the effect it was now having on his wife and daughter, to himself and Fallon in the blink of a very angry woman's eye.

She was pacing now, and glaring over at him with every pass. "Fallon, I don't expect, or want, any woman to cow-tow to me or follow meekly in my wake," Chad smiled maddeningly, using her own words to infuriate her further.

It was small of him, but Chad loved seeing his woman with all her fiery spirit fairly shooting daggers at his heart. It was both impressive and strangely arousing.

"Oh don't you?! Don't you just!" Fallon snapped out, coming to a stop at his feet and glaring down at him. "You demand that I marry you, state that we'll have a couple of kids right off and maybe a third in time, then can't understand when I say no!"

She flung up her hands and spun around to resume her pacing. "But then, you're a man, you expect women to fall into line and at your bloody feet – so why am I even thinking about it?!"

"Could it be because you love me?" he asked with an infuriating grin.

That stopped her dead in her tracks – his arrogance, she decided, knew no bounds.

"You are the most insufferable man I've ever met,"

Fallon told him, her voice dangerously quiet her temper now white hot.

In one lithe movement, Chad got to his feet and came to stand toe to toe with her. "I'm only insufferable to you because I'm right, and you know it."

He caught her hand when it whipped up to slap his damnably handsome face and said, "I didn't demand that you marry me, I asked you to – my mistake. It would seem I've been too polite, too careful around you for your own good."

When her eyes flashed Chad knew a moment of exquisite torture as he reined in his need to take her in his arms and crush his mouth to hers.

"That stops right now!" he told her, his own anger bubbling viciously beneath the cool exterior.

"You arrogant bastard!"

When she pulled to release her hand from his grip he didn't try to restrain her as she'd anticipated, and fell back a couple of steps as a consequence.

"You have no idea." Chad spoke coldly, softly, his face a picture of disdain. Then, without another word, he left her there, open mouthed and staring after him in mute frustration.

"Oh, you insufferable pig!"

He heard Fallon actually stamp her foot in temper and

grinned all the way up to his bedroom. It was amazing how inspired he felt, and Chad opened up his laptop to vent some of it into his writing.

The following morning, sat at the breakfast table, Chad told Fallon that they needed to go to the city to run an important errand for her mother.

Fallon frowned up at her mother who was busying herself with washing up the breakfast dishes. "Why does he need to go – I'm perfectly capable of driving myself?"

Turning from the sink, Mrs Craemer wiped her hands on a tea-towel and smiled at her mutinous daughter. "I know you are, Fallon, but I'd like Chad to take you," she insisted gently. "Apart from anything else, it will do Chad good to get out for a while, give him a complete change of scenery."

Rolling her eyes to the ceiling, Fallon huffed, "And we all want to do what's best for Chad!"

While Chad managed to hide a smile, Mrs Craemer didn't hide her disappointment at her daughter's lack of manners. "Fallon Craemer, I did not raise my daughter to be so rude and unfeeling! Chad has kindly offered his services in this matter and you will go with him – I'd never forgive myself if he had an accident on that blessed motorway, and him only just getting back on his feet."

Feeling foolish and properly rebuked, Fallon nodded

her agreement. "Ok, sorry, I just didn't see why I couldn't do it on my own."

"Well, that's settled then," and Sheila turned back to the sink to finish the washing-up with a satisfied smile on her lips.

Less than an hour later, Fallon climbed into Chad's car and sat stiffly looking out of her side window, refusing even to look at him.

He didn't even try to make conversation, but left her to stew in her own petulance.

It didn't take long, however, before Fallon turned in her seat to put the radio on – the silence in the car was deafening and uncomfortable.

When she sneaked a look at Chad, Fallon saw that he was quite relaxed and had the glimmer of a smile tugging at his gorgeous lips that only served to annoy her even more.

"What are you so happy about?" she demanded sullenly, hating the petulance in her voice but just too out of sorts to do anything about it.

"The sun is shining, I'm actually getting out and about and I have a beautiful woman at my side – what's not to be happy about?" Chad grinned companionably.

Ignoring his infuriatingly chipper tone, Fallon frowned over at Chad. "How come you're driving anyway – I thought you had to get clearance from the hospital before you were allowed to get behind the wheel again?"

"Yes, and I did," he told her pleasantly. "They were very pleased with my recovery and gave me a clean bill of health."

That wasn't entirely true. They had been very pleased with his recovery but had cautioned Chad not to over-do things and to listen to his body when it told him he'd had enough and needed to rest.

"Not enough of us do that..." the consultant had told him sagely "...and we pay the price for it in the long run. I can't count the amount of patients I've seen, over the years, who have ended up in a car accident or mangled a part of their anatomy in some sort of machinery just because they didn't listen when their bodies told them they needed to take a break."

Sitting up straight in her seat, Fallon stared at him as if he'd suddenly grown a second head. "Why didn't you tell me – we're supposed to be a couple, damn it?!"

"Are we?" he asked sweetly. So sweetly that it grated on her last nerve.

"You know damn well we are," she shot back. "That means you should have told me you were going to the hospital and I should have gone with you!"

She sat back in her seat with her arms folded tight

across her heaving chest. How did he always manage to do this to her, to wind her up so tightly that she could barely breathe.

"I didn't tell you because you were having one of your snits and I'd asked Matt to drive me by the time you shook it off," Chad told her without any hint of rancour.

She didn't know why, but Fallon found herself having more than her usual quota of 'snits' lately.

The man drives me crazy – one minute he's at death's door and I'm terrified I'm going to lose him, then he's up and doing things like nothing ever happened! How am I supposed to feel when I'm so screwed up with worry and fear – I love him, doesn't he realise that, doesn't he know how much all of this has hurt me, too?

"You could have told me before this," Fallon told him, some of the hurt lining her softly spoken protest.

He glanced sideways, then looked back at the motorway they were speeding along and reached a hand out to take hers. "Yes, I could have, and no doubt should have…" Chad conceded "…and I don't really know why I didn't."

That was a lie, he knew why he hadn't told her, hadn't asked Fallon to go with him to the hospital. What if the news had been bad, the headaches were less frequent but they were still bad at times.

He'd contemplated his future, one that might not have included Fallon – if the news had been bad he wouldn't have put her through whatever the outcome might have been – he'd have finished it to allow her to move on with her life and gone away to let her do so.

But thanks be to God, it hadn't come to that. The MRI scan had shown no significant problems and the jigsaw that was his skull appeared to have healed well.

CHAPTER FOURTEEN

They parked in a multi-storey car park and made their way down to street level.

"I forgot to ask what we're doing here and mum didn't say," Fallon said as they emerged into the sunny day and she shielded her eyes to look up at Chad.

"We're going to your parent's solicitors," he informed her, patting one hand to his breast pocket. "Sheila asked me to bring in the revised will that she and her solicitor discussed over the phone. He sent her the will to check and sign and now we are taking it back to him."

The colour drained from Fallon's face as the implications of what they were doing hit her. "She's dying – my mother has some kind of illness that she hasn't told me about and she's dying!"

Chad rolled his eyes and gave her hand a squeeze at the same time. "Stop jumping to all the wrong conclusions," he rebuked gently. "Your mother hasn't been able to bring herself to put her affairs in order since your father's death. It's just something that needed doing and we're helping to get it done – ok?" he asked, putting a knuckle under her chin so that Fallon would look at him. "Your mother is in fine health, as far as anyone knows."

Her bottom lip still trembled, the terrifying thought having unnerved her completely. "I couldn't bear to lose her, too. Not right after-" She broke off, unable to put her thoughts into words.

"What? What is it, Fallon? You've been so angry these past weeks and it isn't like you," Chad told her, his hand on her cheek and his thumb lightly caressing the side of her mouth.

How could she tell him what his brush with death had done to her? Fallon Craemer, the woman who didn't take crap from anyone and who prided herself on her inner strength and level head had fallen to pieces.

Oh it was all well and good now, when his doctors had given him a clean bill of health – but she had twisted herself into all kinds of knots, fearing the worst in the beginning then fearing the consequences of the injury on any future they might have.

Hell, she'd worried that they wouldn't have a future, that their relationship would break under the strain of it all. Now here he was, asking her what was wrong and she couldn't find the words to tell him.

Shaking her head, Fallon took a step away from Chad and managed to force a smile. "It's nothing, just a panicked thought that caught me off guard. We'd better go in, we're causing a nuisance standing here blocking the doorway."

Going inside the office block, Chad and Fallon walked over to the lift and read the board that listed the companies and the floor they occupied.

"Fourth floor," Chad said, and pressed the call button. "This shouldn't take long, your mother said the envelope just needed handing in at the desk."

The receptionist's desk faced the lift and the smart young woman behind it smiled a greeting to them as they crossed to her.

"How may I help you," she asked politely.

Taking the envelope out of his inside jacket pocket, Chad held it out to the receptionist. "Mrs Craemer asked me to drop this into you – it's for the attention of her solicitor, Mr Fiennes."

Taking the envelope, the receptionist checked it had the relevant details on it then said, "I'll make sure he gets it, thank you. Is there anything else I can help you with?"

But Chad shook his head, disappointing the young woman whose heartbeat had quickened at the sight of him. "No, thank you, just the envelope for Mr Fiennes."

Once outside again, Chad and Fallon made their way back to his car and climbed in.

"You still look sad, can't you tell me what's wrong?" Chad asked, full of concern.

But Fallon only shook her head, pinning on an unconvincing smile in an attempt to hide the pain behind it. "I'm fine, really," was all she said.

Watching her a moment longer, Chad turned in his seat and started the engine. "I know fine well when you're fine and when you're not — when you're ready to talk I'll be ready to listen."

He wasn't angry, but Chad found himself at a loss as to how he should handle this situation. He'd thought Fallon's behaviour strange for a while now, but hadn't paid it too much attention.

She'd always been a strong character, it was one of the things that drew him to her. But Chad had never seen this side of Fallon before, so deeply angry yet unable to vocalise it.

What she was angry about was a complete mystery to him, and Chad had thought long and hard over it. He'd lain in bed after one of their heated discussions and found himself wondering what the hell it had been about.

Fallon stood up for herself, that was a given, but she had never been argumentative just for the sake of it. In fact, in the past they had rarely argued in any serious sense. They had disagreements, sure, but nothing like the biting arguments they seemed to have lately.

If she'd just open up to me, maybe I'd be able to give a little ground and not get on her last nerve as I seem to be doing at every turn.

Damn it, I'm not a bloody mind-reader!

Such was Fallon's detachment from time and place, she didn't notice that they were continuing south on the motorway instead of heading back home. Only the rumble of her stomach drew her out of her musings and then she looked at the dashboard clock.

"Christ, where the hell are we?!" she demanded, turning shocked eyes to Chad.

"Still on the motorway," Chad replied calmly.

"Well I can see that for myself," Fallon snapped. "But where the hell are we going – we would have been home long ago if that's where we were headed!"

"But that isn't where we're headed," Chad smiled.

She closed her eyes and fisted her hands, mentally screaming and desperately trying to get a grip. "I realise that, now will you please tell me where we are going."

He was impressed by her control, something Fallon has lacked for the last little while. "We're going to the airport – I'm taking you away for a while – we could both use the break."

She gasped, looked at him like he'd lost his mind then Fallon did scream. "You can't just whisk me away without asking – I don't want to go on a bloody holiday with you!"

"Why not, you're always saying you want to see something of the world before we settle down. Well, now we are," he told her, his smile sure and relaxed.

"This is tantamount to kidnap," Fallon huffed, turning back in her seat with her arms folded tight across her chest.

Chad couldn't hide the smile that spread across his face. *If we weren't in a car she'd have stamped her foot as well…just as she did as a girl. And what a girl she'd been – no one had been able to steer her from a course of action she'd already decided on, such was her grit and determination.*

She learned a lot of tough lessons from her hard headedness but had never complained. Fallon took her knocks with the best of them and moved on. So why isn't she doing that now?

"That's a bit dramatic, don't you think, when I'm only

taking you on holiday. Most women would love to be whisked away on the spur of the moment," Chad told her, and earned a withering scowl.

"I'm not most women," Fallon bit out angrily.

"No…" Chad shook his head and sighed "…you're certainly not. Perhaps if we get you something to eat your disposition might improve."

Saying that, Chad steered the car off the motorway and into the car park of a Welcome Break service stop.

"What are you doing – just turn around and take me home," Fallon demanded hotly.

Taking the keys from the ignition, Chad replied with just one unrelenting word. "No." Then he got out of the car and made his way towards the smell of hot food.

She sat where she was for a mutinous minute then Fallon got out of the car and slammed the door shut with a resounding thud.

The bip of the automatic locking made her jump, which didn't improve Fallon's mood in the slightest.

"Just bloody wait, I'll report you to the police, I'll call them the minute we get inside," Fallon shouted, not caring who stopped and stared at her.

But Chad didn't so much as turn to look at her or falter in his stride.

She followed him in, and looked around for a

telephone. *I'm going to call Wes, he'll be furious and come and get me. Then he'll no doubt give Chad a piece of his mind for kidnapping me! Bloody heathen!*

Stalking off to the public telephone, Fallon dug in her pockets for change. "I don't believe it!" She didn't have a penny piece on her...not a one.

Well she could hardly ask Chad for change to call her brother, but what else was she supposed to do. So she walked up to where Chad stood in the eatery queue and held her hand out palm up.

"I need some change for the phone," Fallon demanded without preamble.

To her surprise, Chad reached into his pocket and pulled out the necessary coins and put them in her outstretched palm. "Knock yourself out."

Snapping her dropped jaw closed, Fallon turned on her heels and headed back to the phone. Now they would see what was what!

Wes answered his mobile with a cheery, "Hey sis, how you doing?"

"I need you to come get me, that's how I'm doing," Fallon snapped back. "Chad's kidnapped me!"

She felt her blood boil when Wes laughed out loud. "That's just not possible – he's taking you away for a couple of weeks, that's all. You should be thanking him. I hope you're not giving Chad grief just because he wanted to surprise you?"

"But I don't want to go away with him," Fallon complained, but even to her it sounded unreasonable and mulish.

"Don't spoil it, Fallon. Just because he didn't discuss it with you first, which would have spoilt the surprise part of all this, doesn't mean you can't go along with it and enjoy yourself. Just give the man a break," Wes finished on a plea.

"Fine! Just fine! Even my own brother won't help me," Fallon snapped back, and angrily stamped her foot.

"I am helping you, Fallon. You both need some time alone together, this is the ideal opportunity," Wes replied quietly. "Now, be a good girl and behave."

With that he was gone, had put the phone down before Fallon could voice any more protests.

Be a good girl and behave – who the hell does he think he's talking to...a five year old!

By the time she got back to where Chad had been in the eatery queue he was gone. Now she had to cast her eyes about the crowded room until she spotted him at a table near a wall of windows.

"I got you chicken with all the trimmings," Chad smiled across the table at her, not bothering to ask Fallon the outcome of the telephone call. "Eat up before it gets cold," he encouraged, digging into his own meal.

She was sullen and pushed the food around her plate for a minute or so, but after the first grudging bite Fallon tucked in enthusiastically.

While Fallon finished clearing her plate, Chad poured them both a cup of tea from the little stainless steel pot and pushed hers towards her.

"Thank you," Fallon muttered reluctantly, and secretly peered up at him through lowered lashes.

You look tired. I hate seeing you this way. Maybe I should drive the second leg of this stupid journey. He'll have a headache by the time we reach the airport.

Hey, there's a thought, which one are we going to?

"Which airport are we headed for?" Fallon asked.

"Gatwick – it shouldn't take us more than another hour from here," Chad said casually.

"You look tired – maybe I should drive," she told him, and was surprised by the sceptical smile she received in return.

"Hoping I'll drop off to sleep and you can turn the car around to head back home?"

The thought hadn't entered her head, which annoyed her even more than his accusation.

"If that's all the thanks I get for being concerned

about you, then forget it! Only, don't blame me if you give yourself a bloody headache!"

With that declaration, Fallon shoved to her feet and stalked out to wait back at the car.

That bloody, bloody man! Why the hell do I bother? Why? He annoys the hell out of me half the time and the other half...well...damn it...the other half he's Chad, the man I love beyond reason. Probably a good enough reason to get me certified and locked up!

She was so lost in her own angry thoughts that the bip of the car unlocking made Fallon visibly jump.

"Sorry, I just thought you'd want to get in the car before the rain starts," Chad told her, but couldn't quite hide the smile that tugged at his lips.

"What?" Fallon looked up at a grey sky that did, indeed, look like it would open up with a flood of rain at any moment. "Oh."

They climbed inside the car just in time. A deluge of fat raindrops battered the windscreen and rattled off the roof causing a deafening din.

"Jesus, where the hell did this come from?!" Fallon demanded with nervous hands covering her ears.

Chad knew Fallon didn't like storms and hoped it wouldn't turn into a lightshow. But he was doomed to disappointment when a clap of thunder rent the air, followed by a bolt of lightning that forked down from a very angry looking sky.

"Holly hell!" Fallon scrambled into Chad's lap and clung to him like a limpet. "It's going to hit us any minute now...it's going to hit us, Chad!"

With Fallon's head buried against his neck, Chad held her tightly, enjoying natures display and the side benefits of having his woman willingly clinging to him.

"It won't hit us – it's moving away," Chad assured her as Fallon tried to burrow inside him.

"Doesn't sound like it to me." Then she jumped and clung even tighter when a massive clap of thunder seemed to rock the car.

"We could make a run for it and get back indoors," Chad suggested, but didn't really think Fallon was up for that, and had his suspicion confirmed when she said, "Are you crazy!"

The storm was an unholy flash in the pan – one minute the sky was being lit up and cracked with thunder loud enough to wake the dead, then it was gone and the sun was peeking through the grey clouds as they began to dissipate.

It took a minute for Fallon to trust that it was really over, or that's what she told herself when she reluctantly climbed off Chad's lap and back into her seat.

"Can we just go now?" she asked, irritable with herself and wanting to be doing something, even if it was complying with Chad's travel plans.

"Your wish is my command," he smiled, and smoothly edged the car out of the parking lot and back onto the motorway.

"If that were true we would be going the other way," Fallon stated broodily, but it was a token protest as she was coming round to the idea of time away from the farm.

Chad seemed to sense the slight shift in her mood and only smiled at her observation. Fallon would stick to her guns on principle, but she was coming around.

CHAPTER FIFTEEN

Venice. He hadn't told her till the last minute where they were going, and now she stood looking out over the Grand Canal, in awe and speechless.

"It's beautiful, isn't it," Chad smiled as he watched Fallon drink it all in. "We can go for a gondola ride, if you'd like. Or take one of the larger tourist boats and listen to the tour guide's rendition of the history of Venice."

Suddenly, completely out of the blue, Fallon's eyes prickled with tears and she had to struggle to fight them back. "Why did you do this? Why did you bring me here?"

He heard the tears in her voice and moved closer to Fallon to circle her waist with his arm. "I brought you here because you've talked of Venice as one of the places you most want to see, and I wanted to be the one you saw it with for the first time."

He pulled Fallon round to face him and put a gentle hand to her cheek. "Stop fighting me, Fallon, and let yourself enjoy this trip, you'll only regret it if you don't."

He'd done all this for her, arranged the whole thing just to please her, and Fallon finally gave in to the sweetness of the gesture.

"You really did all this for me," she asked, tipping her head to one side in a curious gesture. "Why?"

"Does there have to be a reason? I love you, we've been through some rough times lately and I wanted to give this time to both of us."

She had a million and one questions to ask him like, how did you get my passport and who packed my suitcase, but none of that was important right now.

"I love you, too." It was that simple, and Fallon had to marvel at the realisation. She still couldn't let go of the unreasonable tension that kept a firm grip on her insides, she'd had it ever since the attack that had almost taken Chad from her. But it did seem to ease, just a little, and Fallon leaned into Chad on a sigh of capitulation.

It was late, the lights of the surrounding buildings were reflected like jewels scattered on the canal's inky surface while gondolas took couples on romantic boat rides.

"Tomorrow will be soon enough," Fallon whispered softly while her hand began popping the buttons of Chad's shirt. "Tonight is just for us."

He didn't need any more invitation than that. Chad closed his eyes and let the feel of her hand, roaming over his now bared chest, flow through him till it stirred his blood.

The physical side of their relationship had never been a problem – they were two passionate people, hot blooded in every way and delighted in giving as much pleasure as they took.

His lips were tender as they trailed over Fallon's face and down to her ear, his teeth nipping at the lobe before his tongue pushed inside.

She shivered and groaned, as Chad had known she would; Fallon's ears were extremely sensitive to his erotic ministrations.

There was no rush in their movements, no hurry to end the exquisite pleasure of tasting bared flesh and the joy of revealing more.

If the gods had given them just one thing that they were both attuned to, it was this ability to understand the needs of the other and the deep desire to sate them.

Fallon moved around him, her hands never leaving Chad's well-toned body, until she stood at his back and smiled with admiration.

His muscles were well defined, his buttocks high and firm, and she couldn't resist nipping at every dip and curve as she worked her way down his body.

She felt his shudder, loved the way her man responded to the anticipation she built in him. Fallon knew how to rouse Chad, how to make him want her until it was almost painful and wasn't surprised by his groan when her teeth sank into his buttock as her hand reached around to hold him.

He was so hard, his pulsing length filling her hand as she worked him, slowly at first then harder and faster until Chad growled at the effort to hold himself back.

"Damn it, woman!" Chad whirled around, lifted Fallon and heaved her onto the bed in one fluid movement. Then it was her turn to moan and scream as Chad dove between her spread thighs and speared his hot tongue into her.

Her breathing was ragged, her body alight with sensation and need and so close, so very close to taking that first tumble that would shatter every nerve ending her eager young body possessed.

"Now, Chad, now!" Fallon demanded, fingers pulling at his hair in an effort to force his compliance.

As he rose over her their eyes met, all heat and flame and insane with need.

"You're mine," he stated roughly, drawing her hands up and holding them above her head. "Say it – I want to hear you say the words, damn it!"

A tremor of something akin to panic stole over Fallon for just a hesitation of time, and then she spoke the words he demanded of her.

"I belong to you, with you, always."

Then he was inside her, the hard length of him plunging deeply, so deeply and so hard that Fallon wanted to hold on to Chad's arms while she pistoned her hips up to meet him, but he still had them pinned above her head.

His roar was animal like, the muscles of his body bunching and trembling like an earthquake moving through him when Chad finally exploded into her.

She felt it to the core of her being, her man driven wild by her body and Fallon responded to him in kind. The shudders that spread from the heat of her sex to the tips of her aroused breasts were so strong they stole her breath. That first explosion of pleasure, almost painful in its intensity, then rippled out all through her body.

"Chad...Chad..." she moaned his name like a prayer.

They clung together, limbs entwined and fell into an exhausted sleep. The combination of stress, travel and a strenuous bout of extremely satisfying sex had wiped them both out, and neither moved till morning.

Fallon opened her eyes and couldn't think where she was or how she had gotten there, but after the first shock of disorientation it was 'his' scent that settled her.

She was clamped around his hard body, gone soft with sleep, head laying on his steadily rising and falling chest.

They were both still lying on top of the quilt, only now it was pulled over them too.

Chad must have woken in the night and wrapped us up snug as a bug in a rug, Fallon smiled dreamily.

His breathing changed and Fallon knew the moment Chad awoke.

"What time is it?" he asked dully.

"I don't know and don't care," Fallon snuggled in deeper. "We're not moving, and that's that."

"Alright by me," Chad willingly agreed, his arm tightening about her.

They lay like that, each lost in their own thoughts, satisfied just to be so perfectly fit against each other.

Then Chad's stomach let out a loud protest and Fallon couldn't help giggling.

"It would seem your stomach thinks it's time to get up after all." Fallon leaned up on an elbow, smiling down at Chad. She watched him, the fist in her stomach tightening its grip as Fallon marvelled at the fact that Chad was here, he hadn't died, the doctors had been wrong.

She felt his hand on her cheek and turned into it. "What's wrong, Fallon – I just watched you go from happy to pensive in the blink of an eye – can't you tell me?"

"It's nothing," she told him, but the forced smile wasn't convincing.

His stomach gave another growl and this time Fallon pushed out of bed and stood with a hand outstretched to Chad, an invitation to get up.

"Come on, we'll take a shower together then get your noisy stomach some food," Fallon grinned.

She was back, whatever had troubled Fallon had been pushed to the back of her mind, and Chad decided to let it go.

"Such a bossy woman," Chad told her, taking her hand and allowing Fallon to pull him to his feet. He stood tall and lean, both of them naked as the day they were born. "I think I need to assert some authority around here," and so saying, Chad bent, lifted Fallon off her feet and slung her over his shoulder.

She shrieked then battered at his back with her fists. "You idiot, put me down!"

But Chad was enjoying himself too much to relent. He strode into the bathroom and the double shower cubicle then turned the water on full.

It was cold, and Fallon kicked her legs and pummelled

his back while she screamed blue murder and promised to carry it out.

"Chadwick Langdon, I'll throttle you just as soon as I stop shivering," Fallon told him, standing rubbing her arms in the now warm water.

He laughed, a carefree sound that melted Fallon's heart, only she wasn't about to let him off the hook that easily.

"I don't know what came over me – the doctors did say I might act rashly, or be prone to sudden mood changes," Chad told her, his look of innocence not fooling Fallon for a moment.

"Oh really. Well think on this, Chad Langdon – I will get you back for freezing me half to death. Not today, maybe not tomorrow, but I will get you back," Fallon promised, her eyes glinting wickedly. "Be afraid. Be very afraid."

Taking a step back, Chad looked at her as though he was taking her seriously. "You would make a terrific villain – that threatening look is very convincing."

Fallon's mouth tipped at the corner as she raised one brow. "You can mock, but I will prevail."

They ordered room service and ate their breakfast on the balcony.

"This has to be a dream," Fallon said, sitting back in

her chair, her stomach full and sighing contentedly.

"I'm glad you're enjoying it," Chad smiled, he loved to see her so relaxed and happy. "We could take a water taxi to St Mark's Basilica, it's said to be one of the finest examples of Byzantine style architecture – they literally brought columns and statues from other countries and meshed them into the existing structure."

"Yes, they were certainly creative," Fallon agreed. "I'd love to see it."

When they stepped outside of the hotel, Fallon had to shield her eyes from the sun glinting off the water.

They made their way over to what was essentially a gondola car park and were greeted by smiles and invitations to 'come sit'.

Getting into the gondola wasn't as precarious a process as Fallon feared. Chad held one of her hands and the gondolier held the other until she was safely seated.

After he had told the boat man where they wanted to go, Chad laid his arm along the back of Fallon's shoulders and pulled her into his side. "There isn't a more romantic city than this, I shouldn't think," he observed, marvelling at the sights and sounds that surrounded them.

"It is beautiful – but real, if you see what I mean," Fallon smiled and tipped her face up to look at Chad.

"Yes, it isn't picture perfect, but the flaky paint on the

exterior walls doesn't detract from the overall feel," Chad nodded in agreement.

Their journey was deliberately slow, giving them the time to look around and enjoy the ride.

Music was wafting on the warm breeze, light and appropriate to the setting. Fallon saw a little girl leaning out of a window and waving at the gondola's as they passed by. Lifting a hand she returned the wave and the little girl grinned happily, babbling something in Italian.

When Fallon frowned the gondolier smiled. "She wished you much love," he told her and Fallon blushed at his sexy Italian tone.

"Thoughtful girl…" Chad grinned and took hold of Fallon's hand in her lap "…let's not disappoint her."

She couldn't fault the gondolier, he kept the boat moving and their ride smooth and she was almost disappointed when they pulled up to the mooring closest to the basilica.

"Thank you, that was truly amazing," Fallon told the smiling gondolier as he helped her out and onto dry land.

"Welcome, pretty lady," the smooth Italian blew her a kiss, even though Chad was yet to alight the boat.

But Chad knew it was just their way, an expected flirtation that thrilled most women and probably had them looking out for a particularly charming gondolier thus earning him more business.

They walked through to St Mark's Square hand in hand and both were delighted by what they saw.

The large piazza was impressive in architecture, size and atmosphere. There were as many pigeons as there were people, if not more, and the noise of their fluttering wings and low calls was louder than you might imagine.

People not only stood in family groups chatting about their day, but many had their heads tipped back looking at the buildings and the beauty they held.

There was not one blank unadorned wall – most had intricate mouldings and columns as well as ornate windows that sparkled in the sunlight.

"Can we just sit," Fallon asked, wanting to take the time to let it all sink in.

He was delighted by her response and steered Fallon over to a nearby bench. "It is awe inspiring," Chad agreed as he sat beside her. "There's no rush to do anything – just relax and enjoy."

She did. Fallon watched and listened, allowed herself to absorb the atmosphere and to imagine what life might have been like for earlier inhabitants.

"Even the prison looks ornate..." Fallon eventually observed "...though I don't suppose the accommodations were any less austere than any other prison."

"I doubt it – apparently the Bridge of Sighs, which

connected the prison to the old inquisitor's rooms in the main palace, got its name from the many sighs the prisoners made when they crossed it – never to return to their cells," Chad finished with a spooky air.

Fallon rolled her eyes but didn't resist the smile that tugged at her lips. "Well I read something quite different," she declared. "The name, 'Bridge of Sighs' refers to the sighs lovers make as they pass beneath it in their gondolas – and, comparing the two stories, I prefer my version."

"You would," Chad chuckled. "I think I do too," he added, putting an arm across Fallon's shoulders and pulling her in for a tender kiss.

Reaching up, Fallon placed a delicate hand on Chad's cheek and simply stared into his loving eyes.

"Do you want to sit here a little longer, or perhaps you'd like to see inside one of these lovely buildings," Chad asked, his voice low and rolling over her like a lover's caress.

"You are a very special man, Chadwick Langdon. I've done nothing but give you grief these last weeks and you brought me to Venice," Fallon declared, her smile rueful. "I'm going to try to even the balance and enjoy our time together in Venice, so we'll start with St Mark's Basilica and work our way round this lovely square from there, ok?"

CHAPTER SIXTEEN

It was like being on an unofficial honeymoon, Fallon decided when they got back to their hotel and dressed for dinner in its restaurant.

Chad was dressed in a charcoal dinner suit while Fallon wore a dress she had never seen before.

"I doubt my mother or my brother bought this dress, so that leaves you," she told Chad when she stepped out of the bedroom and into the sitting room where Chad sat waiting for her.

"Quite right," he agreed, coming to his feet to get a better look at her. "And, if I say so myself, I have brilliant taste – you look stunning."

She watched his eyes travel slowly up and down the full length of her body and felt the response that she always felt when Chad looked at her in just that way.

The frisson of sexual tension that shimmered through her left Fallon breathless and damned near made her tremble.

"That sapphire blue brings out the colour of your eyes and makes your blonde hair look like a halo," Chad murmured as he walked towards Fallon. "And this silk…" he put a hand to her waist and let it slide slowly down her hips "…makes me want to run my hands all over you."

"Then we'd better get out of here before I take you up on that," Fallon told him on a shaky laugh.

The dress was full length sapphire silk with a tantalising slit at the side that stopped 6 inches above her knee. It was sleeveless and held up by one strap that widened out to form the diagonal bodice which barely hid the shape and form of her lush breasts beneath it.

Chad didn't think there was a single eye in the room that didn't turn to admire Fallon when they entered the restaurant. Not all the stares were admiring, some were downright green with envy, but even they had an edge of reluctant admiration about them.

There was no doubt about it, Fallon was the belle of the ball and she was his!

The maître de hurried to them and showed them to their table, his smile and bow overly solicitous.

"What the hell is wrong with people…?" Fallon asked, her blue eyes wide and confused. "I feel like I just walked into the room naked!"

Chad chuckled softly and took her hand. "Oh no, my love, but what you did was much more enticing," he told her and chuckled again.

"Then you'd better tell me what I did so I can make sure not to do it again," Fallon frowned.

A waiter handed them both a menu and the conversation turned to food. "Thank heavens they have English translations," Fallon commented as she looked at the range of meals available.

"That's because they know we English are too damned lazy and ignorant to take the time to learn other languages," Chad told her with a sigh. "And I'm no better than the many others who have come before me – I don't speak a word of Italian, or any other language come to that."

"I managed GCSE French, but I doubt I could hold a conversation in French now," Fallon mused, then shrugged her lovely shoulders. "Until I live in a different country English will just have to do me."

"So you'd learn the lingo if you lived somewhere else?" Chad asked with real interest.

The waiter returned and took their orders then Fallon answered his question thoughtfully.

"I'd think that was essential – wouldn't you?" she frowned over at Chad.

"There are lots that don't bother," Chad replied. "That's why there are so many ex-pat's communities in Spain, Italy, and no doubt lots of other countries – we move there and then expect to live the same lives we lead in England, language and all."

"Would you do that, if you lived abroad?" Fallon asked with genuine interest. "After all, you could do your work anywhere there's electricity to plug your laptop into."

"True, and I have thought about it," Chad replied, surprising Fallon.

"You have – but I thought you were all about marriage and family," Fallon eyed him dubiously.

"Again, true – but not right away," Chad clarified and watched Fallon's brow crease in thought. "I want to marry you more than anything, but children are not an immediate requirement. I'd like to take my stories to an international level – go to different places and incorporate them into my work."

The meal arrived and Fallon found herself eating it without much thought. Her mind was replaying Chad's original marriage proposal and comparing it to what he had just told her.

How can he say those things now – he was so determined to settle down and get married and his plans definitely included at least two children!

It didn't make sense that he would just change his mind on a whim – not Chad.

But was it on a whim? Chad hadn't started writing his books until he'd taken off after she'd refused to marry him – maybe that had influenced his thinking.

Or maybe it was something more recent than that – a good crack on the skull might have addled his brains, but she didn't really believe that. Chad had worried about that also, but there had been no outward signs of change that she had noticed.

No, if Chad has changed his mind about marriage and children, it's to do with something else entirely. But what?

Continuing to mull it over, Fallon ate her meal and drank the fine wine that Chad had ordered, barely registering them.

The waiter came to clear their dishes away and handed them the sweet menu, making Fallon look up at him in surprise.

"You've been lost in thought – care to share them with me," Chad asked as Fallon turned back to him.

"I...I'm not sure," Fallon hesitated, not convinced that she wanted him to know how seriously she had been considering his marriage proposal. If children really were something for the future...

"Then let me take a stab at guessing," Chad smiled, taking a sip of his wine before wading in. "Firstly, you're probably wondering if I'm in my right mind – considering the blow to my head I can't blame you for wondering," and she blushed which gave Chad his answer.

He nodded and gave a rueful smile. "I must admit, it was a very real worry for the first couple of weeks. However, the headaches are getting less frequent and are not so intense, so there's an improvement."

"Chad…you say that like it was nothing." Fallon had to swallow back the resentment and the tears that were building at the back of her throat. "You almost lost your life, how can you be so blasé about that?!"

The waiter smiled as he delivered their sweets, seemingly oblivious to the tension in the air.

"May I get you anything else?" he asked pleasantly, but gave a little bow and left when they both said, "No, thank you."

As if they had never been interrupted Chad shook his head and took her hand. "I didn't mean to sound blasé," he told her, giving her hand a reassuring squeeze. "But I don't like to dwell on what could have happened – it didn't and that's all to the good as far as I'm concerned."

She closed her eyes, feeling the fist in her gut squeezing and twisting until it was almost unbearable. Pushing her untouched sweet away, Fallon picked up her wine and drank it with trembling hands.

"Tell me what's wrong," Chad asked, his voice low and

pleading. "You've been like this since I came out of the hospital. Have you fallen out of love with me – because if you have I'd rather you didn't stay with me out of pity?!"

Her bottom lip began to tremble and the tears in her eyes shone bright as diamonds. "That's a bloody stupid thing to say – I might know you'd have no idea."

Pushing back her chair, Fallon threw down her napkin and rushed out of the room. Chad sat dumbfounded, not a clue what he'd done or said to account for her behaviour.

Chad finished off the wine then moved into the lounge where he continued to drink steadily for the rest of the evening.

What the bloody hell had she meant by that – of course I don't have any idea what she's thinking if she doesn't bloody well tell me – I'm not a bloody mind reader, am I?

His thoughts went round in circles and became more confused the more he drank.

Been in a bloody bad mood ever since I came home – worse than she usually is, damn it. It's not like I asked to be hit over the head, and why should that make her mad – it was my bloody skull that got cracked like a flaming egg!

Trying to get to his feet, Chad stumbled sideways a step then sat back down heavily.

"Let me help you sir," a waiter offered, taking Chad's elbow as he made to stand a second time.

"Women, can't live with them and can't live without them," Chad declared seriously, eyeing the young man who was now guiding him towards the lifts.

"No, sir," the waiter agreed.

"You got one?" Chad asked abruptly.

"Oh yes sir," the waiter smiled. "My wife is expecting our first baby very soon," he proclaimed proudly.

The lift door opened and the waiter entered the lift along with Chad. "I will see you back to your room, Mr Langdon – this hotel is so big you might get lost."

Chad narrowed his eyes suspiciously at the young man. "You think I'm drunk," he stated rather than asked.

The waiter did a fine job of keeping a straight face but felt the corner of his lips twitch. "No, sir. As I said, this hotel is very large, easy to get lost in if you are not familiar."

Saying goodnight to Chad once his key card had been inserted successfully, the waiter watched him go inside before pressing for the lift doors to close.

She'd left a table lamp on, but Fallon was nowhere to be seen. "Probably gone to bed with the bloody hump," Chad told the empty room. "Well, so bloody what, I'm not a bloody mind reader – can't understand if she doesn't tell me what the bloody hell's going on, can I?"

He fell face first onto the settee and only then did Fallon come out of the bedroom where she'd been listening to his drunken ramblings. She rolled him onto his side and took his shoes off, then she undid the top two buttons of his shirt and went off to get a blanket.

"You idiot man," Fallon told Chad as she laid the blanket over him, but smiled as she took a seat beside him. "I could never fall out of love with you – though you drive me to distraction with very little effort."

Her fingers gently combed his chestnut hair back from his face then caressed his cheek.

"You gave me the fright of my life when I thought I would lose you, and the anxiety still won't leave me," Fallon whispered, her hand laid gentle and still against his cheek. "It grips me at the oddest times, like tonight in the restaurant. I couldn't bear it, that you could flick off the danger you had been in, it was like you were flicking off my feelings – it hurt, Chad. It really hurt."

CHAPTER SEVENTEEN

When Chad woke on the settee next morning, his head felt like it had been split open again and the pain was crushing.

"Bloody hell," he groaned as he sat up and cradled his head in both hands.

"You did a lot of that last night," Fallon informed him, but Chad didn't even look up, he couldn't.

"A lot of what?" he asked quietly.

"You used the word 'bloody' a lot," she told him with a grin. "You're really suffering aren't you?"

He heard the grin in Fallon's voice and managed to raise his eyes long enough to scowl at her.

"You had the fun, now you have to pay for it," she told him. "I'll ring down for some Alka-Seltzer."

After making the call to room service, Fallon crossed to the complementary tea and coffee and made them both a cup of coffee.

"Here you go." Fallon pushed the strong black coffee into his hand and sat watching Chad try to keep his head from falling off his shoulders.

"It's really bad, isn't it?" Fallon asked unnecessarily, but with a hint of sympathy that seemed to soothe Chad.

"The worst," he told her.

"Maybe it's worse because of your head injury – I imagine any headache will hurt worse than usual for a while," she suggested.

He made to nod his head, then thought better of it.

When someone knocked the door, Fallon crossed the room and thanked the waiter. "You're a lifesaver," she grinned.

Chad had barely touched the coffee she'd made him but reached for the Alka-Seltzer eagerly and polished it off in double quick time.

"Not sure I should have done that." Chad held a hand to his stomach and grimaced.

"If you're going to throw up, please do it in the bathroom," Fallon told him brusquely.

"Thanks for the sympathy..." Chad frowned "...but I think I can manage to keep my guts where they are."

"Good, because housekeeping would not like the clean-up job," Fallon reminded him, then walked out onto the balcony to sit and watch Venice wake up.

It was still early, only around 7 a.m., but the gondoliers were already setting up in readiness for another busy day on the Grand Canal.

Chad had pulled on sunglasses before joining Fallon on the balcony. "Not a view you could tire of easily," Chad commented as he took the seat next to her.

"I couldn't agree more," Fallon smiled warmly as she took in the idyllic scene. "Let's just relax today – have meals on the balcony and watch the world go by."

He knew she was thinking of him, and Chad had to be grateful for that. "Let's just see how the day pans out – if my throbbing head winds down to a bearable level we could go out this afternoon, maybe."

"It's not important," Fallon assured him. "I could sit and watch this view for hours on end and not have enough of it. This place is so lovely, and this hotel is perfectly placed to enjoy it. Thanks for bringing me here, Chad – I've neglected to say that."

Leaning back in his chair, Chad reached out a hand to take Fallon's and held it while they sat in companionable silence.

As it happened, they didn't venture out in the

afternoon. Instead they enjoyed room service and each other's company.

It had been a long time since they had done so, and it felt strange to realise that.

"It was almost worth getting a hangover to spend the day with you like this," Chad told Fallon as she snuggled into his side on the settee.

"Almost...?" Fallon tipped her face up to look at Chad and smiled at his grimace.

"Well it was hellish painful," he reminded her. "That'll teach me to lay off the whiskey when I'm in a mood."

"Yes, and don't you forget it," Fallon wagged a finger at him then leaned up to kiss Chad's pursed lips. "I don't like to see you suffering, it hurts me too."

That surprised him. Just the naked truth in the simple statement filled Chad's heart with hope for their future.

"Then maybe you should marry me to keep me on the straight and narrow," Chad smiled, but his eyes told her that he wasn't joking.

"Is that the best reason you can come up with?" Fallon asked, tipping her head to one side the better to see him.

It was the last thing he had expected to be doing that day, but Chad got up and went to the bedroom to get the small box that he'd brought with him...just in case.

Walking back into the sitting room, Chad stopped in front of Fallon and dropped to one knee.

"I can think of a thousand reasons why we should get married, but none of them better than the simple fact that I love you…soul deep, and always will.

You are the most precious part of my life – the part that made fighting for my life a necessity and not a choice. I want a life with you, Fallon, and one day, when you're ready, I want children to complete our family."

He grew silent, watching Fallon in fear she might storm out or just refuse him out of hand, but when she didn't, Chad opened the little box and continued.

"Fallon Craemer, if you would do me the great honour of becoming my wife I can promise you the world would be your oyster. We can travel and see as much of it as you'd like – all I ask is that we do it together, as man and wife. Will you marry me?"

When she didn't immediately say yes, Chad began to lose hope. Then Fallon took his face between her gentle hands and said, "There isn't a woman alive who could love you more than I do right now."

Her eyes gleamed bright with tears and love.

"Becoming your wife has been my dream since I was old enough to realise what it meant, and probably even before that," she smiled. "Yes, I will be your wife and we will have children…in time," she affirmed gently. "In the meantime I'm sure we'll enjoy practicing to make them."

He bowed his head, overwhelmed by Fallon's acceptance, and had to rein in his emotions.

With fingers that he had to will to be still, Chad took the diamond solitaire ring out of the box and gently put it on Fallon's wedding finger.

"You've made me the happiest man alive," he told her, and Fallon could see that he truly meant it.

"How's your head?" she asked with just a hint of a smile.

"Feeling much better than it did this morning."

Fallon stood and held out her hand to help Chad to his feet then kissed him soundly on the lips. "Then I think it's time you took me to bed – I want to feel my fiancé's hands on me."

There was no rush or hurry to remove clothes or climb into bed, both of them were happy just to touch and be touched and to kiss and be kissed.

When he'd lain near death in his hospital bed, this had been the dream that had kept Chad alive.

She was going to be his wife – that thought alone had Chad walking on air and needing to please Fallon, to give her everything that he was and could be.

When he caressed her skin it felt like velvet, when his

lips tasted her breasts they were as nectar to a bee. He suckled and stroked, nipped and teased, and her response humbled him, made him want to give her so much more.

"You're so beautiful, Fallon. You make me weak with wanting and strong as a lion because you want me back," he crooned, his hand cupping her heat and finding her already wet.

When his fingers slipped inside her, Fallon's head fell back on a long moan of pleasure. He had been the only man to touch her in this way, the only man she had ever wanted to touch her in this intimate and secret way.

The pleasure of one ignited pleasure in the other, fuelling their passion until it begged to be sated.

But Chad wanted all, touch, taste and capitulation of his woman. His woman – the thought made him hard as rock and he throbbed with need.

At any other time, Fallon might have felt the need to assert herself, to take back some vestige of control, but not now. Her lover was staking his claim, with every touch he was saying 'you are mine' and Fallon understood, opening for him willingly.

This was a joining like no other. When Chad pushed inside her, Fallon gasped out a single word… "Yes!" …and Chad understood, driving himself into his woman again and again.

Now they moved in unison, she bucking beneath him, he thrusting to meet her urgent need, a need that was building to a violent crescendo.

It shook them both to the core of their being, was so profound that all they could do was cling to each other until it passed.

They fell into sleep still locked in each other's arms, sank into the blissful peace of the loved.

CHAPTER EIGHTEEN

They walked, hand in hand, through the streets of Venice, their contented smiles telling all who saw them that they were a couple in love.

"You know, we need to savour this calm in our relationship..." Chad smiled at Fallon as she tipped her face up to look at him "...because, let's face it, we enjoy riding a good storm, don't we?"

She laughed – actually threw her head back and enjoyed the release of it. "We do. We really do. But, life would be boring if it were all plain sailing, wouldn't it?"

"For us, I think it would," Chad agreed. "Your fire is what I love about you – that instinct you have to challenge the status quo if it doesn't suit you."

"That sounds like a convoluted way of saying that I'm

argumentative," Fallon frowned, but was smiling as she did so.

"It did, didn't it?" Chad grinned. "But what I really meant to say is, you're fearless in your self-belief – I admire that about you."

She still wasn't sure that it was a compliment, but the day was beautiful and Fallon was loath to spoil it with an argument.

"Hmm, well, as long as you keep on admiring me, I'll let the rest pass," she told him, and felt Chad give her hand a gentle squeeze.

"So, now that you've agreed to marry me, shouldn't we talk about the time and place for the service?" Chad asked, trying not to sound like he was in a rush. Which, of course, he was.

Knowing Fallon as he did, Chad wouldn't put it past her to prevaricate or even to change her mind. But he didn't think she would once the family were informed of their engagement.

It made him want to take her home immediately. To whisk her off to the airport and catch the next flight back to England.

Suddenly, that was all he could think about and his blood raced with excitement.

Even before Fallon could answer, Chad said, "Let's go

home…right now…let's just get on a plane and go tell our families the good news."

He held the hand he was holding up between them and gazed down at the large solitaire diamond he'd put on her wedding finger. Then he bent his head and kissed it, as if sealing an oath.

"I love you, Fallon, I want the world to know it," he said when Fallon remained silent.

It was really just a moment's hesitation, but it was enough to send Chad's heart racing. Surely she wasn't going to go back on her promise to marry him?

Then she nodded. Just a small movement, and a smile began to pull at her lips. "Ok…" she agreed, sounding a little stunned "…we can do that."

Then she was being lifted up in the air and spun round and round as Chad let out a happy laugh.

"We're getting married," he announced when passers-by stopped to look at them.

Many clapped and congratulated them; one woman took a rose from a bouquet of flowers she was carrying and handed it to Fallon, the flood of Italian that came with it going right over their heads, but the meaning had been clear.

'Love is a beautiful thing, nurture it well and enjoy.'

Fallon looked at Chad over the rose as she held it to

her nose and sniffed it. "This is real," she told him, as though that fact had only just sunk in. "All that fearless self-belief you were just crediting me with, it just flew out the window – I'm terrified," Fallon admitted.

"But not of me. Not of us," Chad stated confidently, touching a hand to her cheek. "The rest is just something we have to do for the family – though, hopefully, you'll enjoy your big day as brides usually manage to do."

"Bride," Fallon repeated, almost to herself. It was like an alien concept that she was having trouble associating herself with.

"Yes, bride," Chad grinned, enjoying Fallon's rare uncertainty. His woman was usually absolutely sure of her footing and strode along life's pathway knowing exactly where she was going and why.

But not today. Today Fallon seemed to be having difficulty getting her head around the idea of marriage, of becoming a bride.

He didn't doubt that Fallon loved him, but Chad was nervous that she might turn tail and run if she thought he was trying to clip her wings, or put her in a 'wifely' box that might grow to feel like a gaol.

"Marriage isn't about putting shackles on each other..." Chad said softly, his thumb gently caressing her cheek "...it's an affirmation and commitment to our love…to our life together, wherever that life and love may take us."

Her hand came up to cover his and, at last, Fallon's mouth pulled into a smile. "I love you, Chad. I know that without a shadow of a doubt, and I have to trust that love or I'll end up doubting everything that I am, and I've never done that before."

"We're going to do a lot of things we haven't before," Chad nodded. "I'm not a millionaire yet but, according to my agent, my book sales are going through the roof and I've had a very lucrative offer for my next book. We can travel wherever you'd like – as you said before, I can work anywhere there's a plug for my laptop."

The nerves about marriage were suddenly washed away by the flood of excitement about their future together. "There's so much I want to see and do – but being able to do it together will make it all the more special."

They took the time to do a little shopping – something special for the two mothers and smaller mementoes for everyone else.

Fallon drank in the loveliness of the city for the last time, enjoying the gondola ride back to their hotel.

"We'll come back," Chad told her when he came up behind Fallon as she stood gazing out over the Grand

Canal. Slipping his arms around her waist, Chad pulled her back against him and they enjoyed the view together.

"I don't think I want to," Fallon said, surprising him. "I want to remember Venice just like this, the place where you proposed and I agreed to marry you. It's perfect."

She felt his arms tighten about her then turned within them to face the man she had committed her future to.

"Make love to me, Chad, I want more memories to take home with me."

If there was one thing that they were entirely attuned to, it was each other's bodies and the pleasures they were capable of giving and receiving.

When his hands caressed her, Fallon knew an intense pleasure that shimmered under her skin awaiting his next touch. When that touch came, the ripples from it seemed to excite every nerve ending until she was quivering from it.

Only Chad could give her this, only he had ever made her want to feel this way, made her want to give herself over to him completely.

Their lips met in a kiss that was deep and demanding, fierce and gentle all at once.

"Fallon..." Her name whispered from his lips as they moved over her face with reverence, kissing first her eyes then working his way back to her luscious lips and on down her neck to the racing pulse in her throat.

Chad was in no hurry, he too wanted to savour the memories they had made together in Venice, and this one would be the best of all.

This act of love would seal their promise to love each other for the rest of their lives.

There was nothing that Chad would not do for her, and he did everything to pleasure his woman in as many ways as he knew how.

Fallon writhed beneath him, moaned out his name and climaxed time and time again. When he took her, when he plunged hard and fast between her welcoming thighs, Fallon clawed his back and Chad groaned as the exquisite pain shot through him.

Their final climax ripped through one and into the other, a tumult of physical need and emotional acquiescence.

They were joined in every way possible but one, and soon they would be one in the eyes of God.

<u>CHAPTER NINETEEN</u>

Having texted Matt that they were back in England and would be heading for the Craemer's farm first, Chad drove out of the airport's long term parking and headed up the motorway towards Dersley Dale.

"Still excited to tell your family about our engagement?" Chad asked, turning briefly to gauge Fallon's expression.

"Of course – why are you looking at me like that," Fallon asked, looking aggrieved. "I'm no coward."

"I didn't say you were," Chad corrected. "But you do look nervous."

She frowned at the fast flowing traffic and considered. "Aren't you even a little bit wary of all this? I mean, once we tell everyone...well...I just have a feeling that things will go a little crazy. Do you have any idea what goes into a wedding?"

"My Brother got married recently, remember," Chad chuckled.

"Yes, and I helped Pam with the organising – it was a nightmare," Fallon huffed. "Well, I enjoyed it some of the time, but that's when Pam was the bride."

"And you don't think you'll enjoy it when you're the bride?" Chad asked quietly.

She heard the regret in his voice and felt truly awful. "I didn't say that...exactly. I just..." Breaking off, Fallon turned in her seat and looked at Chad with pleading eyes. "Couldn't we just elope? I'm serious," she added when Chad looked doubtful. "I have no objection to us getting married...but all that fuss...it should be just us," Fallon tailed off, knowing she didn't stand a chance of getting her way.

"You really want to run off to Gretna Green?" Chad shook his head, mystified.

Blowing out a breath, Fallon shrugged her slim shoulders. "I don't know about Gretna Green, but I do wish we could just do it and then tell them all."

She was serious, Chad realised. He'd always assumed that brides liked big weddings – white dress, bridesmaids and a church.

"If that's what you really want, that's what we'll do," Chad chuckled softly, shaking his head in wonder.

It didn't matter to him, truth be told he was of the same mind. It was all about them making their promises to each other, they didn't need to do so in front of a crowd to make it any more real.

"Are you serious?!" Fallon gaped at Chad like he'd grown two heads.

"If that's what you really want then that's what we'll do," Chad assured her.

They were still about an hour away from the turnoff towards Dersley Dale, so Fallon decided she had some time to think it through.

It's not like the family haven't already had a get-together, Pam and Matt's wedding saw to that.

But would my mother be disappointed – I'm the only girl and mums get all gooey over their daughters getting married.

It would be great though. Just me and Chad making our vows then taking off on our honeymoon.

She sighed heavily and Chad covertly looked over to see how Fallon was doing. He knew she was having a tough time working things out in her head – it's what she always did. As much as Fallon wanted to elope, she would take everyone else's feelings into account first.

"Damn it!" Fallon exclaimed suddenly. "We can't do it – much as I would love to cut and run, my mother would be devastated."

"Alright, you decided what kind of wedding you want, I'll try to make sure that's what you get," Chad assured her.

"Really – just like that," Fallon frowned suspiciously.

"Why not?"

"Because you're no bigger fan of fuss and ceremony than I am – how come you're being so agreeable?"

Chad's smile was wide and easy as he turned to glance Fallon's way. His hand reached out to cover hers in her lap as he said, "My dearest wish is to marry you – the how and where is up to you, just as long as you turn up."

She blinked at that. *What a thought, as if I'd leave him standing at the altar – surely he doesn't really believe that?!*

"Are you worried I'll get cold feet?" Fallon asked eventually.

"No. Of course not." But Chad did secretly have concerns along those lines. "You've given your word and I have no reason to doubt you."

But she heard it in his voice. Chad wasn't as confident as he wanted to appear.

The turnoff was just moments away and when Chad

turned off the motorway Fallon felt a moment of panic.

"Bloody hell," he heard her mutter and knew just how she felt.

Why did families go so over-the-top when it came to weddings? The mothers fussed over dresses, flowers and colour choices, while his father would be getting all nervous over giving a speech.

Wes would no doubt step in for his father, walking Fallon down the aisle and giving the speech their father would have made.

It was another reason that Chad had been happy to consider eloping. Not having her father there to give Fallon away would only rub in the fact that he was no longer with them and might rub salt into a still open wound.

Fallon and her father had been close, Chad knew that. It had broken her heart when he'd died.

"It's all going to be fine," Chad reassured Fallon as they pulled up outside of the Craemer farmhouse. "Decide what you want and stick to it – you don't usually allow anyone to bulldoze you into doing something you don't really want to."

Turning in her seat, Fallon looked at Chad with desperate eyes. "Would you be happy with a register office ceremony?"

"I've told you, whatever you want will make me happy." He leaned over and kissed Fallon, putting a hand to her lovely cheek. "It's just one day out of our lives – we can give them that, ok?"

Fallon nodded and let go a long sigh as she alighted the car and came to Chad's side.

When they entered the kitchen, Sheila Craemer turned then gasped with surprise. "I didn't expect you back so soon," she told them with a warm smile. "Are you two alright?" Sheila asked tentatively.

They knew what she meant – were they a couple again or had the trip to Venice only driven them even further apart.

Moving forward, Fallon held out her left hand and watched her mother dab at her eyes with her apron.

"You're engaged," was all she could manage through the sudden onset of tears.

Fallon wrapped her arms about her mother's neck and chuckled softly. "I rather thought you might be happy for us...or are these happy tears?"

Returning her daughter's hug, Sheila looked over her shoulder to Chad and said, "I'm very happy."

Then a voice from the doorway had Fallon pulling back to grin at her brother. "What's going on – you two didn't elope, did you?"

Chad and Fallon looked at each other and smiled at their secret. "As if we'd do that," Fallon chided her brother, not giving anything away, and then Ashton came in behind Wes.

"Who eloped? You did not!" Ashton gasped wide eyed at Fallon then Chad.

"No, we did not," Fallon rolled her eyes, then held out her left hand for Ashton to get a look at her ring.

"Bro, that is a serious rock," Ashton raised an eyebrow at her brother. "What did you do, rob a bank?"

Chad just pushed himself away from the doorframe where he'd been leaning and sat down at the kitchen table. "What can I tell you...book sales are good."

"Did you set a date yet?" Ashton asked, now full of questions and putting her arm through Fallon's in a companionable girly way.

The two girls made their way up to Fallon's bedroom for a more in-depth talk, leaving their men to worry what plan's they would cook up between them.

Sheila Craemer put the kettle on, as was her habit when any visitors arrived. The fact that it was her own daughter and her fiancé, oh she loved the thought of that, made no difference at all. It gave her hands something to do while she acclimatised to the good news.

"I dread to think what they're talking about up there,"

Wes said as he took a seat opposite his best friend.

"Doesn't really matter, does it?" Chad asked with a raised brow. "It's all about the bride, so we might as well let them do whatever makes them happy, right?"

"Right," Wes agreed, but his nervous frown in the direction of the two women's laughter made his agreement somewhat unconvincing.

"I do know that Fallon doesn't want anything too big or fancy," Chad informed Wes and his mother casually. "I just hope Ashton isn't trying to push her into having a big white wedding."

"Would that bother you?" Sheila asked.

"Yes," Chad answered immediately. "Not for myself, but I want Fallon to have the wedding she wants, not something to please everyone else."

Nodding over the mug of tea she had served at the table, Sheila considered silently for a moment. Looking at Wes she said, "Remember how she was about school photos and birthday parties?"

"I do," Wes smiled. "Fallon hated being the centre of attention and threw a wobbly all damn day."

"So much so that we gave up having parties for her after she was six — the tantrums just weren't worth it," Sheila shook her head at the memories.

"Sounds like you wouldn't mind if we had a small

family wedding?" Chad observed, looking from Sheila to Wes with a question in his eyes.

"Not me," Wes shook his head and looked to his mother. "You?"

"In truth, I think Fallon takes after me – your dad and I didn't have a big wedding either," Sheila confessed. "We'll go along with whatever you and Fallon want," she told Chad with a smile.

"Got any idea on the when part?" Wes asked.

"Soon as pos'," Chad told him. "I don't want to give Fallon the chance to get nervous and back out," he admitted.

Surprisingly, Sheila nodded her understanding. "That's a possibility, and not because she doesn't want to marry you," she assured Chad. "Fallon builds things up in that head of hers and scares herself silly – that's what she used to do as a child. Sooner is definitely better."

No sooner were the words out than the two young women, who had been laughing earlier, walked back into the kitchen, their faces all serious.

Chad actually had to swallow back his nerves.

"We've come to a decision..." Ashton announced, smiling at Fallon, their arms still hooked together, "...and we want to get married together...on the same day," Ashton added as if to clarify the matter.

Fallon remained silent but nodded in agreement.

Wes almost choked on his tea and Sheila reached across to smack his back.

Chad chuckled at his friend's shocked reaction then turned and looked to the two young women who appeared to be in control of the situation. "So, you want a joint wedding – I can get behind that. What else did you two decide?"

It was Fallon's turn to step up, and Ashton gave her a less than subtle nudge. "Well, we decided we don't want to wear white – at least, not the fluffy wedding dress type of thing. We were thinking that maybe we could just wear something eveningy – like a nice cocktail dress...or something," Fallon frowned, imagining herself having to get dressed up for the big day.

"And we don't want lots of people – just family and close friends," Ashton put in when Fallon didn't continue.

"Got a timetable for all this?" Chad asked, relieved that nothing outrageous had been thought up by his often hare-brained sister.

"We do," Ashton grinned at Wesley, noting his silence and his pallor. "As it will only be immediate family and friends, we thought we could get it organised in around a month-"

"A month!" Sheila Craemer almost shrieked the words out.

"They're kidding," Wes frowned at his mother and then at the two young women. "You're just kidding, right?"

Both girls shook their heads in unison and Chad thought Wes might do something really embarrassing, like passing out from shock.

"I doubt any marriage could be arranged that quickly," Chad offered, giving Wesley's shoulder a friendly thump. "But we could probably pull it off in 6 weeks."

Wesley's mouth worked but nothing came out.

"Even that would be pushing it," Sheila Craemer said, considering everything that would need doing.

"28 days," Ashton stated stubbornly. "We looked it up on the internet," she smiled sweetly.

"Are you trying to give me a heart-attack?" Wesley finally found his voice. "Why all the rush – we haven't even discussed any of this with your parents?"

He thought about Charley – he'd be bound to think that Ashton was pregnant at this rate. Then it hit him.

"You're not...you're not..." He just couldn't get the final words out.

"Not what?" Ashton asked, then took a step back when the penny dropped. "Wesley Craemer, how dare you suggest I'd Shanghai you into marriage!"

Chad knew his sister of old and moved to cut off her

explosive temper before it could get a head of steam on. "That isn't what he meant at all – but it's something dad will wonder at," Chad warned his sister.

"Then you'll set him straight!" Ashton looked at Wes expectantly.

"Of course – but you have to admit, it does look fishy," Wes offered.

"They could think the same about me," Fallon offered. "We just want to get it done – no fuss, just family and friends and a marriage license."

"Suits me just fine," Chad smiled over at Fallon, and got a beaming smile in return.

"Looks like you're outvoted," Ashton grinned at Wesley and moved forward to wind her arms about his neck. "Not really upset about it, are you?"

Blowing out a big sigh, Wes shook his head. "Christ all bloody mighty, Ashton – why don't you just hit me over the head next time, it can't feel any worse."

Then Wes realised what he'd said and turned to Chad. "Bloody hell, I'm sorry, I didn't think…"

"Don't worry about it," Chad chuckled, fingering the scars on his scalp. "But I can assure you, it feels a hell of a lot worse than being verbally poleaxed."

The release of tension had everyone laughing, if a little nervously.

"So, is that the plan sorted then?" Sheila asked, looking from Ashton to Fallon and from Wesley to Chad, watching as they all nodded. "Then we are going to be very busy from this moment on. I gather we're talking registry office wedding and a small reception after?"

"We thought we could have finger food and drinks here," Fallon told her mother. "Between the sitting room and the kitchen, there's plenty of room for people to mill around and sit."

Sheila looked dubious. "Exactly how many people are you thinking of inviting?"

"Literally just close family and a couple of friends," Fallon assured her. "Fenella and Jackson and Mac, of course." She turned to Ashton with a quizzical frown, "Anyone else?"

"Nope, that about does it. I made it 12 people in all, and that includes both brides and grooms," Ashton smiled with some satisfaction.

"We're going to ask Pam to be Matron of Honour with Lizzy as a bridesmaid." Fallon smiled now the shock of their announcement had worn off.

"Pam will love that and Lizzy will be thrilled," Chad grinned, amazed that this was really going to happen.

CHAPTER TWENTY

Pam and Lizzy were both thrilled at the news, if a little taken aback by the short notice.

"You're a pair of crazy women," Pam laughed at Ashton and Fallon sat in the sitting room of the Langdon farmhouse along with Lizzy.

"Not really, we're keeping it simple and enjoying our day with the people who really matter to us," Ashton dismissed airily.

"We're all going shopping tomorrow – I've already cleared it with Matt," Fallon told Pam and Lizzy. "You've only got one group riding lesson booked in and Matt is going to take that."

"Well," Pam gasped, then looked at Lizzy who was grinning happily.

"It's exciting, isn't it?" the young girl declared.

"That's the spirit," Ashton laughed.

"Ashton and I thought we'd buy an evening or cocktail dress – something simple but dressy enough to show that we care about the significance of the day," Fallon stated. "And we thought you and Lizzy would like to choose something similar – perhaps coordinate your outfits so that you feel part of the wedding."

Suddenly, Lizzy looked worried.

"What is it, Lizzy?" Pam asked quietly.

"I've got some money saved, but I'm not sure it'll be enough for this," she murmured, embarrassed.

"Don't be silly – Fallon and I will be going halves with the expenses and both yours and Pam's dresses and shoes are included," Ashton told her.

"They are – you're not just saying that...?" Lizzy asked shyly, looking around the group of women.

"Not at all," Fallon assured her. "We asked you to be bridesmaids, why should you be out of pocket because of it?"

"I suppose," Lizzy smiled, taking the explanation at face value. "It'll be the first time I've ever been shopping for clothes – mam usually does all that sort of thing."

Pam remembered the few clothes Lizzy had had when she'd first started at the stables and smiled. Most of those had been replaced by clothes that Pam had altered to fit her, and Lizzy had been thrilled to have them.

Not that Lizzy didn't have her pride, it had taken some cajoling to get the young girl not to see it as 'charity'. By telling Lizzy that they no longer fit her and suggesting that it would be a waste just to bin them, Lizzy had agreed to let Pam take them in for her.

"Actually, I can't remember the last time I went shopping for myself," Pam put in. "We could make this a real girly day – go shopping and have tea and cakes in one of the little tea shops afterwards."

"What do you think about inviting Fenella to come along with us?" Fallon asked cautiously.

The young woman had suffered a lot of torment from the press since she'd handed over some damning evidence against her newspaper owning father.

As Fallon had warned her might happen at the time, the police had taken out a search warrant that had allowed them to search Theodore Swain's home.

The fallout from Fenella's action had been her father's arrest and her mother's desertion. The woman had actually taken Fenella to task over the shame she had brought on the family and had then moved out of Dersley Dale and gone to live permanently with her sister in Scotland.

"I feel sorry for her," Lizzy said, sadly.

"Me too," Ashton agreed. "The more I've gotten to know her the more I've come to like her – and what she did, going to the police like that, well, it took real guts."

"Jackson is really gone over her," Pam stated. "The press started hounding him too once they realised about their relationship. They practically mobbed him when Jackson went into the village for a pint – he hadn't a clue the word was out on him and Fenella."

"Do you think it will last?" Ashton asked curiously.

"What, Jackson and Fenella," Fallon asked, and got a nod from Ashton. "I do, yes. Jackson has more backbone than to allow the press to run him off – if anything, he's become more protective of Fenella and spends quite a bit of time over there."

"What...sleeping there?" Ashton gasped.

"The press have been relentless – Fenella didn't feel safe with only the live in staff," Fallon explained.

"I've talked to her when she's come to the farm to see Jackson," Lizzy put in. "She's always nice to me."

"And why shouldn't she be – you're a very nice person, Lizzy," Pam proclaimed.

Lizzy blushed and dipped her head, allowing the conversation to go on around her. She still felt shy in company but was getting better at joining in.

The shopping trip was full of fun. Fenella had gratefully accepted the invitation to join the expedition to the neighbouring city and the five women had a ball.

The brides started off trying on conservative evening dresses, long sheaths that were truly stunning but not what either was really looking for.

"I'm not sure what I want, but I know I don't want a traditional wedding dress." Ashton screwed up her nose at her reflection and turned to the other women seated nearby. "You know what…" she continued with a mischievous grin, just as Fallon emerged from the changing room "…I feel like having some fun with this."

"What have you got in mind?" Fallon looked cautiously after her future sister-in-law as she headed for a completely different section of dresses.

"How about this?" Ashton was holding up a stunning mini dress in navy lace with see-through panels in strategic places.

At first, the girls laughed then frowned uncertainly when they realised that Ashton was serious.

"Well, you'll certainly make an impact in that," Fenella grinned. "You'll knock Wesley's socks off."

"That's the idea," Ashton laughed excitedly, turning to Fallon with a dare in her sparkling green eyes. "Let's both give them something to remember," she challenged.

Hesitating for just a moment, Fallon's grin widened to match Ashton's. "Hell yes! If we're going to do this we'll do it our way."

Lizzy looked at Pam, her expression asking the question, *Do they expect us to wear dresses like that?!*

Pam discretely shook her head and watched Lizzy blow out a sigh of relief.

The dresses the two young women tried on went from daring to almost non-existent.

"Ashton, you wouldn't," Pam exclaimed when the younger woman emerged in a dress so short she would barely have to bend over to show off her underwear.

Walking over to the mirror, Ashton turned this way and that admiring the way the high heeled sandals and the shortness of the gold dress exaggerated her long legs.

"I'm tempted," she grinned back at Pam through the mirror. "I could wear this when we go clubbing on our honeymoon."

Pam looked at Fenella and the other woman just shrugged. "It's their day, if they want to liven things up they're certainly going the right way about it."

Then all eyes turned to Fallon – the only traditional thing about the dress she wore was the fact that it was white. "What do you think?" she asked them while doing a slow turn.

Ashton gaped, then nodded enthusiastically. "You look stunning – like a bride with attitude!"

"That's what I was going for," Fallon laughed nervously. "I really like this one."

It was white lace over a bikini lining that left the midriff sheer. The sweetheart neckline emphasised her pert breasts and the corset-style stays added structure to the waistline. Like Ashton, Fallon had long legs that looked stunning in the high white court shoes she wore to match the very short dress.

"Ok, I'm going to look for something similar – white with attitude," Ashton laughed, and heard the other girls laughing as she danced off to scour the rails.

A young, female attendant had been rehanging the dresses the women had discarded and watched the fashion parade with interest. Never had she seen brides like these before – but she had to admire there daring.

"Ok, this is the one," Ashton announced as she emerged from the dressing room again and began a slow turn to show off the dress.

The asymmetrical bodice had a single wide strap that was encrusted with different sizes of diamante bling. It continued down the back and widened out to form a translucent sparkling panel that was attached to a white skirt, low on one side and higher on the other. A sheer panel of matching sparkling gems crossed from underneath Ashton's right arm to the top of her left thigh where the skirt panel began. A matching white panel covered her full breasts from the right shoulder strap to her left side.

"You look amazing," Lizzy said before she realised what she was saying.

The four inch white strappy sandals had matching bling and the whole effect was one of sexy opulence.

Fallon got up from her seat next to Fenella and the two women crossed to stand side-by-side in front of the large mirror and grinned.

When they turned back to their audience every one of them agreed that they looked amazing. Even the young shop attendant was nodding and smiling enthusiastically.

"Looks like you're up," Fallon said, looking from Pam to Lizzy, who suddenly looked scared. "Don't worry, Lizzy, you can wear whatever you feel comfortable in. Just enjoy trying on whatever you like – and no looking at the price tags," Fallon warned.

Pam and Lizzy didn't take half as long as Ashton and Fallon had in choosing their dresses. They settled on powder blue as the colour theme and both dresses were very conservative.

Lizzy's was a plain, short sleeved, square necked, A-line dress that came down to mid-calf length. It looked lovely on her and made her look older than her 16 years.

Pam's was the same shade of powder blue but had a more grown up sweetheart neckline that highlighted, but didn't over emphasise her bust-line.

The girls were all having a ball, laughing and twirling, teasing and cooing. Lizzy had never before enjoyed herself so much.

Even Fenella got in on the fun, declaring that she would need a new outfit for attending the wedding, or risk being shown up by everyone else.

Her dress was a beautiful autumnal rust colour with exquisite gold embroidery detail.

They took their bags and boxes and loaded them in the boot of Fenella's car before going for their 'girly chat', over tea and cakes.

"Good job I brought dad's Land Rover, we'd never have got it all in else," Fenella chuckled happily.

"I've never seen so much shopping," Lizzy said, goggling at the packages they'd carefully stowed in the Land Rover's boot.

"Well, Lizzy, it's all had to be done in a bit of a rush – we only have three weeks left until the big day," Ashton grinned, putting her arm through Lizzy's.

"Will it all be ready – seems a lot to do in such a short space of time," Lizzy said, looking up at Ashton.

"Easily," Ashton stated confidently. "Fallon and I don't want a lot of fuss – it'll be a quick trip to the register office then home for a party with family and friends."

They piled into a quaint tea shop and queued up to place their orders. "This is on us," Ashton said, leading the way. "All part of the wedding expenses."

"Go on, Lizzy, I'm sure they taste every bit as good as they look," Fallon told the young girl who was ogling a fresh cream fancy.

Unable to resist, Lizzy put the amazing cake onto a plate and then put it next to the glass of cola she already had on her tray.

They filed past the woman sat behind the till and let her see what they had. When she'd totted up the bill, Ashton paid it and joined the rest of the girls at a table in the far corner.

The chatter was happy and the laughter loud at times, but no one seemed to mind.

"You should go in for a spray tan," Fenella suggested to Fallon and Ashton. "There isn't time to use a sunbed – even the fast tanning ones will only give your skin a bit of a glow."

Ashton and Fallon looked at each other and nodded. "The white dresses would look stupendous against a golden tan," Ashton agreed.

"Alright, but I think I'd rather get it about a week before – give it time to fade a bit and look more natural," Fallon said, thoughtfully.

"Hmm, and you don't want any residue hanging around to stain the dresses," Fenella nodded in agreement.

Lizzy looked on in amazement, she'd never heard of a spray tan. It sounded messy and had to be embarrassing to have applied – you'd surely have to be naked, after all.

"What about you lot – don't you want to have a St. Tropez tan?" Ashton asked, looking around the table at Pam, Fenella and a very reluctant Lizzy.

Pam declined, saying she was happy with her own natural colour. Which was softly golden due to the hours she spent out of doors.

Lizzy agreed quickly, saying that her mam would probably skin her alive if she got to hear about it, and it wasn't like she'd be able to hide it.

"No, I'm happy the way I am for now – though I'm looking forward to a holiday in the sun sometime soon," Fenella chuckled. "I'm still trying to talk Jackson into flying – I can't believe he never has!"

CHAPTER TWENTY-ONE

The weeks that followed were filled with intense rounds of debate and stress.

Sheila Craemer worked with Avis to organise the food, each bringing different ideas and skills to the table.

"I could make the wedding cake…" Avis offered "…it would have to be sponge rather than fruit, but I can make it look like the real thing."

"Oh that would be lovely," Sheila agreed. "Do you have any ideas for the theme?"

"Not really – I'll try to get some ideas from the girls," Avis smiled, loving all the preparations that a wedding entailed.

"Will they want a cake each, do you think?" Sheila asked.

"Hmm, I'll ask the question but for so few guests it seems a bit of a waste," Avis frowned.

"Yes, and they'll have other things to eat as well," Sheila added.

"When Fallon mentioned 'finger foods' did she give you any idea what she had in mind?" Avis asked.

Shaking her head, Sheila got up and put the kettle on the stove ready for another cup of tea. "Not really, but I got the feeling both girls were talking about sausage rolls, and the like. But we could always come up with a few ideas of our own."

"I think we can manage something better than a plate of sausage rolls," Avis rolled her eyes in disgust. "This is a wedding, for heaven's sake."

"What did you have in mind?" Sheila asked as she placed a fresh cup of tea in front of Avis, then sat to drink her own.

"I remember your savoury flans, Sheila – I know they'd go down a treat," Avis grinned.

"Ok, I'll make 3 savouries and a couple of sweet ones," Sheila agreed with an enthusiastic smile.

Avis suddenly looked wistful and Sheila asked her what was wrong.

"Nothing's wrong – far from it," Avis sighed, her eyes still misted with old memories. "Our children are getting married in less than a week now – I always wondered if their friendships would come to something more with time."

Sheila's eyes lost focus too, as she recalled her own memories of their children's happy childhood. "I must confess, I always hoped they would," Sheila admitted. "Chad is just what Fallon needs – he's strong and firm but has a deep and abiding love for my daughter that she returns whole heartedly."

Picking up her tea, Avis sipped contemplatively. "The same could be said for Wesley and Ashton – she needs a firm hand but one that won't clip her wings just yet. I think Wesley's already proved that he is more than accommodating when it comes to letting Ashton do what she needs to."

Sheila sighed and looked over her teacup at Avis. "It was a shame about her exit from the showjumping arena – she could have gone all the way, I'm sure."

"I talked to her about it," Avis said, placing her empty cup back in its saucer. "Ashton just said that it wouldn't be the same without Fonteyn as she was the reason she competed in the first place."

"They had an extraordinary bond," Sheila nodded.

"In all my years I've never seen anything like it," Avis agreed with a winsome smile. "From the day Charley gave her that foal they were inseparable. We had the devil's own job getting her to sleep in the house and not in the barn with Fonteyn – though she did so a couple of times when the mare got ill with colic, or some such."

"I did wonder if you'd think Wesley too old for Ashton – I must admit, their age difference did give me a few concerns at first," Sheila admitted.

But Avis shook her head firmly. "Not in the least. Wesley is one of the kindest, most considerate men I've ever had the pleasure of meeting, and he loves Ashton like no one else ever could. I saw that when he came to speak to us about their relationship – when he asked Charley for his permission to propose to Ashton."

"He does. He really does," Sheila grinned happily.

"Ashton said they plan to live here," Avis said, watching Sheila for her reaction to the plan. "Will you be happy with another woman permanently in your kitchen, Sheila?"

"We'll get along well enough," Sheila smiled. "And when the little one's start coming along, I'll be able to help them out a bit. Truth be told, I can't wait."

The two women laughed and nodded enthusiastically, and that's how Charley found them.

"What's going on, you two cooking up wedding plans?" he asked with raised brows.

The two women looked at each other with knowing eyes and put their talk of grandchildren on hold for the time being.

"We're just trying to work out what food the girls will want for the small reception party," Avis told him. "Sheila's going to make some of her flans – that should keep you and the other men happy, at least."

Charley's expression brightened as he smiled down at Sheila. "Can't do better than your savoury pastries," he told her sincerely. "I'll look forward to tasting them, that's for sure."

"Should I be offended by your enthusiasm?" Avis asked, tipping her face up to look at her husband with a suspicious frown.

"Not at all. Not at all. You're a dab hand in the kitchen, and you know it. But Sheila's flans...well..." Charley sighed, letting the thought hang in the air.

The two women watched him go outside, Charley's expression still soft with the fond memories of Sheila's cooking.

When they looked back at each other the two women burst into peals of laughter.

"I'd say that idea was a hit," Avis said as she dabbed at her eyes with a tissue.

"Stay for dinner," Sheila invited, enjoying the company of her oldest friends and not wanting to let it end yet. "I have plenty in and we could cook it together," Sheila offered.

Avis looked out of the kitchen window and watched her husband as he talked with Wesley – it had taken him a little time, but Charley had come around to the idea of his baby girl getting married.

"We'd love to," Avis smiled happily. "I enjoyed seeing a bit of the world, but nowhere compares to home and friends."

The women spent a companionable couple of hours baking and getting the dinner ready, while Charley and Wes got some of the manual work done outside.

It really was like old times, Avis thought fondly. The two families had always been close and the children had benefitted greatly from it.

Both mothers had been used to feeding the other's children, making them welcome just like one of their own. A quick phone call to let each other know where their children were and what they were doing was all it took for things to run smoothly, and they always had.

Whether they were at the Craemers or the Langdons, both sets of parents had always known their children would be safe and well fed.

Now their families would be united in a way that was more binding and, hopefully, would see another generation of children growing up on the farms.

<u>CHAPTER TWENTY-TWO</u>

It was horrendous – three days before the wedding Fenella had been summoned to the local police station for questioning by a Metropolitan police officer who had travelled up from London.

Jackson had gone with her, but he hadn't been allowed in the actual interview room and had sat outside worrying.

Did they think Fenella had been involved with her father's dealings? If so, why on earth would she have come forward with the evidence she found – it just didn't make any sense.

But that Detective had looked severe and suspicious to Jackson's mind – not at all grateful for Fenella's help as the local police had been.

I didn't like the look of him, all brass buttons and a ton of starch in his uniform, Jackson thought, his anxiety level going up when a uniformed officer came out of the room, crossed to a desk then took a folder back into the room with him.

She's been in there for nearly an hour already, what the bloody hell is going on?

He began to pace, glaring at the door as if he could will it to open and Fenella to walk out through it.

They hadn't even stated their reasons for wanting to interview her, he recalled. *Just a terse phone call and an offer for a couple of uniforms to pick her up and bring her in to the station. Like I'd let that happen,* Jackson thought angrily.

His long legs continued to pace, his mind inventing all kinds of scenarios that might be going on behind the closed doors that his eyes kept flicking to.

When Fallon and Ashton walked in through the outer doors, Jackson felt the gratitude for their support wash through his strained muscles.

"Is she still in interview?" Fallon asked with some surprise.

"She is," Jackson told them, his large hands pushing back through his tousled hair. "I'm about ready to go in and fetch her out – it's not right questioning her like this."

"I'm sure it's not what you think," Ashton put a hand to his arm to offer reassurance. "They might just need more information – confirmation of her father's whereabouts at certain times – that sort of thing."

Suddenly Jackson looked hopeful, clinging to the suggestion like a drowning man might to a life belt in a stormy sea.

"Yes, that could be it," he gasped, standing still to look from one woman to the other. "They might just need her to verify dates and facts that they've been collecting – evidence that they're still putting together."

But when the door opened and Fenella stepped out a full half an hour later, it was obvious that the situation was more dire than any of them had thought.

She looked tired, washed out and very sad. When Fenella turned to Jackson her eyes were glistening with unshed tears.

"What the hell's been going on?" Jackson demanded as he crossed to her, taking Fenella in his arms.

"Ms Swain has been very helpful," the London Detective told him, then turned to Fenella. "We'll talk again soon. Goodbye, Ms Swain." Then he walked off without a backward glance and disappeared through a set of doors at the other end of the grim corridor.

Jackson looked at the local police officers for answers

as he felt Fenella tremble in his arms. "Ok, let's have it — why does he need to talk to Fenella again?"

"Ms Swain will be a witness for the prosecution," the Dersley Dale detective informed him sheepishly. "It was felt, by some, that Ms Swain's cooperation in this way would go a long way towards countering any suspicions of her involvement in her father's dealings.

His snarl was almost feral as Jackson eyed the detective through hate filled eyes. "You mean you used that threat to force her into testifying against her own father!" He was angry, so bloody angry that he could have rammed his fist into the detectives face if it weren't for the woman trembling in his arms. "She came to you. Fenella found all that information about her father's dealing and she did the right thing — she brought it to you!"

"I realise that, and we appreciate everything that Ms Swain has done," the detective told him in a placating voice. As Fenella raised her head from Jackson's shoulder, the detective smiled at her kindly. "We really do appreciate everything you've done and we'll do all we can to make this process as painless as possible."

"Fat chance of that!" Jackson spat out before Fenella could reply. "Come on, let's get out of here!"

With that, Jackson spun Fenella round and marched them both out of the police station.

Ashton and Fallon quickly scooted behind them, concerned by the other woman's pallor.

"Jackson, stop," Fallon demanded as he continued to march at a brisk pace, pulling an unprotesting Fenella along at his side. "Are you alright?" Fallon asked when she reached Fenella's side.

She was in a daze, the hammering that the police had given her had left Fenella's mind spinning. "I will be," she managed to whisper just before she fainted into Jackson's arms.

Sweeping her up, Jackson carried her to the car and pressed the key to unlock it. Fallon opened the door to allow Fenella to be seated inside then moved to crouch at the recovering woman's side.

"Fenella? Can you hear me?" Fallon asked with some concern.

"Yes…what happened?"

"You fainted," Fallon told her, taking Fenella's hand and keeping hold of it. "We'll get you home and Jackson will tuck you up for a couple of hours – I think you could do with the rest."

Fenella's eyes searched for Jackson and when she found him she nodded. "Yes, I don't want to think about this awful situation any more. I just want to sleep. I need to sleep," she repeated still sounding dazed.

"We'll come by to see you later," Ashton told her. "Jackson will let us know when you're feeling better."

Jackson nodded. "Could you tell Matt and my father that I'm taking the rest of the day off? I don't want to leave Fenella alone."

"Don't worry about it," Ashton told him, her hand giving Jackson's arm a reassuring squeeze. "You work more hours than you're paid to – Matt won't have any objections, and I'll see that Mac knows too."

The girls climbed back into Fallon's car and watched Jackson drive away with Fenella at his side.

"Christ all bloody mighty," Ashton exclaimed. "I can't think of anything worse – testifying against your own father!"

"Doesn't sound like they've given her much choice," Fallon observed sadly. "Fenella has been put between a rock and a hard place – either she testifies or she'll find herself accused of complicity. Either way, poor Fenella is heading for a rough time of it."

"Well, we'll be there for her," Ashton proclaimed staunchly. "And woe betide anyone in the village mouthing off about her – Jackson will beat them into pulp if he hears them."

Remembering the look on Jackson's face when he'd looked at the detective, Fallon didn't doubt it for a second. "It won't help anyone if he ends up in gaol on assault charges. Maybe you could have a word with Mac to see if he can calm Jackson down."

Ashton nodded as they pulled into Langdon Farm. "I'll go and have a word now, while I think about it."

With that, Ashton strode off in search of Mac leaving Fallon to go into the main house.

Chad was in the sitting room and he smiled appreciatively when Fallon walked into the room. "I can't get over you with that golden tan – you look good enough to eat."

She tried to smile, but it came off as more of a grimace. "I've just been to the police station, Jackson phoned to say that Fenella had been summoned there by a Metropolitan Police Detective who'd come up specially to talk to her."

"Did he say why?" Chad asked, taking Fallon's hand when she sat down next to him.

"They didn't know why, not at the time. The police just said the man had some questions for her and she needed to come into Dersley Dale Police Station immediately. They even offered to send a car to fetch her," Fallon told him, shaking her head in disapproval.

"Sounds like they meant business," Chad observed. "Do you know what it was all about now, or are they still questioning her?"

"No…I mean, yes," Fallon shook her head in annoyance. "No they're not still questioning her and yes I do know what it was all about," she clarified.

"And…?"

"Chad, they're forcing her to testify against her own father," Fallon told him, the horror of that prospect clear in her voice and her sad eyes. "I don't know how she'll get through it – she fainted outside the police station."

He wanted to sympathise, knew Fallon expected it, but he knew a fair bit about Theodore Swain's criminal activities and the man needed locking up.

"It will be hard, no doubt about that – but it needs to be done," Chad told her, and saw the temper flare in Fallon's eyes. "It's no good you getting yourself all worked up over it – Swain is a dangerous man. I doubt he's ever sullied his hands with murder but he's certainly ordered it to be carried out."

She wanted to rise to Fallon's defence, having seen the effect all this had had on her friend, but Fallon had to accept the wisdom of Chad's words, however reluctantly.

"I know you're right," Fallon sighed heavily. Angrily. "But if you'd seen the effect all this is having on Fenella…"

Putting his arm around Fallon's shoulders, Chad pulled her in for a hug. "I've only known Jackson for a short time but, if I'm any judge of character, and I think that I am, he'll stand by Fenella and help her through this. They make an odd pair, don't you think — the farmer and the socialite?"

CHAPTER TWENTY-THREE

Wedding eve was chaotic and both the men and the women alike were looking forward to the evening when all the fun would begin.

Pam, Lizzy, Ashton and Fallon were all staying overnight at Fenella's, so they were busy going back and forth with dresses, flowers and anything else they could think of so that they wouldn't have to return until the wedding was over.

The men had it easy, in Fallon's estimation. They would all be staying at Langdon Farm so they were already ensconced as Wesley still hadn't moved back home.

Jackson and Mac would move out of their converted barn and into the house for the night, but even that was only a mild inconvenience as both domiciles were within a stone's throw of each other.

Charley had said he would stay home with Avis, as she and Sheila had decided not to go to what was essentially the hen do in case they cramped the younger women's enjoyment.

Knowing that Mac would be on hand to stop any excessive drinking or stag-do hi-jinks from going too far, had set Charley's mind to rest.

"I know what our boys are capable of…" he'd told Avis when they'd talked it over "…and I'm including Wesley in that. The three of them can get into more trouble than a dozen men if they've got it on them to do so. I'm trusting that Mac's steadying presence will keep them in line."

Avis had kept her thoughts to herself, she remembered a younger Mac and his ability to tie one on when the mood struck him. He was no angel, but she decided not to point that out to her husband.

If Charley wanted to delude himself into thinking the boys had a good chaperone, it wasn't up to her to disabuse him.

"Did the florist confirm she is going to trim up the register office?" Ashton asked Fallon as they went over the arrangements yet again. "We'll want photos."

As the wedding plans had progressed, it had amazed

the two brides how much they had moved towards a traditional wedding.

At first they had been rebellious, determined to get married their way, but as time went on they realised that having flowers, and a photographer to record the day, were essential elements that they didn't want to forgo.

"She sent me photos of the two standard arrangements to go either side of the signing desk," Fallon informed Ashton. "I thought I showed them to you?"

"You probably did – my head's like a sieve for some reason," Ashton frowned, scratching her head through the thick mane of red hair that tumbled freely down her back.

"Nerves," Pam told her as she passed by. "You're both bound to have them."

Lizzy tried to be helpful, offering to do any little job to get things sorted out for their hen-do later that evening and the wedding the next day.

She'd shown her mother and the boys her lovely dress and shoes and they'd all told her that she looked like a princess.

Her mother was recovering well now, and the boys were doing what they could to help her.

It had been a worry to Lizzy, when her mother had become so ill with pneumonia, but Chad had paid for a home nurse to look after Lucas and Liam while she was in the hospital and then to look after them all for a time when she finally came home again.

Lizzy was still a bit scared of Chad, but not as much as she'd been when first they met. Then she had been terrified of the stern looking man who'd seemed to change moods at the drop of a hat. But Lizzy had grown to respect his judgement and had seen another side to Chad.

He went to see my dad when I was hurt, she recalled, thinking of the day she'd turned up to work in the stables covered in bruises. *I don't know what he said, but dad never hit me like that again. He still clocked me round the ears when he was in a bad mood, but he never hit me as bad as that ever again – Chad saw to that.*

Wary of him, Lizzy might be, but Chad was a hero in her young, adoring eyes.

Fenella had banned them all from the dining room – telling them that she was setting up for the party that night. "I have a theme and you are all required to play along," she told them. "But no one is to look before I say so – alright?"

Everyone agreed. After all, Fenella was the queen of parties in the district. Everyone knew that.

A couple of delivery vans had driven up to the house, one after the other, but Fenella hadn't allowed anyone to see what the packages contained.

"She's enjoying this," Fallon laughed a little nervously, wondering what Fenella was up to.

"I think it's good for her – takes her mind off her father for a little while," Ashton said, and everyone agreed.

"The Metropolitan Police have been in touch with her again – did she tell you?" Fallon asked, looking to the rest of the group.

"Jackson mentioned it," Lizzy piped up. "He said they want her to go to London this time – Monday, I think he said."

"Yes, that's right," Fallon confirmed. "I told her to make sure she had a solicitor with her this time. That last interview was brutal from what she told me – they virtually threatened to charge her along with her father if she didn't do as they asked and testify against him."

"Well, we'll all help her to enjoy this couple of days," Pam stated firmly. "She's keeping herself busy, which is good, and we'll keep her entertained tonight and tomorrow, with Jackson's help."

Ashton caught Lizzy's look of seeming confusion. "What's up, Lizzy, you worried about something?"

The young girl jumped and flushed guiltily. "No. Oh no. I was just thinking, is all."

"What about?" Ashton asked, studying Lizzy curiously.

"I...well...it's just..." She lifted her hands and let them fall back into her lap in a helpless gesture. "I don't have the fancy words that you all do – but I've noticed the way you all are together, the way you really care how each other feels."

Lizzy's flush deepened, as did her embarrassment. "It's just...I've never seen that kind of friendship before. I didn't know being friends was like that."

It struck everyone in the room that what Lizzy had essentially said was that she had never had a friend like that, had probably never had a close friend ever.

"You say that as if you aren't part of our group of friends, Lizzy," Fallon chided her gently. "I, for one, most certainly consider you to be my friend."

When that sentiment was echoed by the rest of the group, Lizzy felt her eyes well up and her bottom lip tremble. "But I'm just a stable girl, I just work on the farm," she stated simply.

"There's no 'just' about it," Pam put in. "You are a very valued addition to the stables, Lizzy, but more than that, you are a much valued friend."

"I didn't realise..." Lizzy told them, sucking in her bottom lip to still it.

"Well you do now, so let's get down to the business of enjoying ourselves," Ashton chuckled.

The men were not so kicked back – they had farm work to see to and business had to continue as usual. Even Chad had been roped in to get all the jobs done so that tomorrow would be a day off for everyone.

"I know how to drive a damn tractor," Chad had told Matt when he'd suggested that Chad might be out of practice.

"You've never driven the new one, and you hadn't driven the old one in a long time," Matt reasoned. "Jackson has a lot of experience with the new tractor, you could help Mac while Jackson takes the feed over to the beef herd."

"If I'm volunteering my services I should get to pick my own damn job," Chad snapped, not used to being bossed around by his younger brother.

"Fine!" Matt gave in. It didn't really matter to him who took the feed out, just as long as it got done. "But if you bang up the new tractor, you pay for the repair bills."

Satisfied, Chad merely turned on his heels and strode out of the house.

"Hey, Jackson…" Chad called to the man who was already beginning to load feed into a trailer "…I'll get that. You help Mac with the Dairy herd, I want a go on her," Chad smiled, nodding to the shiny new tractor.

Returning his smile, Jackson nodded. "Ok. You want me to run you through the controls?"

"Nope – I'll have a play and find them out," Chad chuckled, looking forward to getting his hands dirty again.

Writing books was all well and good, and Chad enjoyed his new career for the most part, but getting your hands into mother earth was satisfying on a whole other level.

He and Jackson continued loading up the trailer with feed then went their separate ways.

Chad climbed up into the cab of the tractor and studied the controls. It was more complicated than the old tractor had been. This model had gizmos and gadgets for doing all manner of things that supposedly made the farmer's life easier.

Turning the engine over, Chad was pleased when it started first time – the old tractor had often taken some persuading to get it going. He wiggled himself to get comfortable and gave the closed in cab the once over.

At least you won't get drowned when it rains, he thought, remembering the times he had been on the old cabless tractor. *Seems a bit like cossetting, but I can't blame Matt for going for the best if the farm can afford it.*

Chad's mind turned back to the trouble Matt had gotten into when Swain had meddled in the farm's finances, forcing creditors to withhold payments owed to the farm in a bid to get Matt under his thumb.

I didn't like the idea of using the lower field for housing construction, but Matt seems to have pulled it off with very little impact on the farm. And at least the farm's finances are ensured for generations to come, if they use the money wisely.

As he drove the tractor across fields, jumping out every now and then to open and lock gates, Chad thought about the unexpected turn his life had taken.

It looked like this was going to be my life when I was growing up here on the farm. I know dad always thought I'd be the one to take over from him, but I always knew Matt had more love for the farm than I did.

He supposed the expectation had been natural enough – him being the eldest – but he'd always had stories running around in his head, even back then.

While he'd been cleaning out the stables, his mind would be thinking up dramatic scenarios that would play out in his head. Not that he'd ever let on. Chad had been a closed book when it came to his personal thoughts and feelings, until he'd found himself falling in love with Fallon.

And hadn't that been a surprise! He'd always thought her bossy, had felt sorry for Wes when she'd bent his ears about something or other he hadn't done, or hadn't done to Fallon's satisfaction.

But there had come a day, around her sixteenth birthday, that Chad had been slammed upside the head with a sledgehammer, it felt like.

At 3 years older than Fallon, Chad had been around 19 when the first jolt of lust for her had punched him in the gut right out of the blue.

All dressed up to go to a friend's birthday bash, Fallon was wearing a dress that showed her curves were developing in all the right places.

She had rarely worn dresses. Fallon had preferred t-shirts and jeans when on the farm, but this was a special occasion.

The parents of the girl whose birthday it was, had hired the church hall and had put a disco on. It was the first grown up event Fallon had been to, but it hadn't been her last.

He'd had to watch her stepping out with one boy after another as other parents followed suit, deeming the discos a safe transition from childish parties to the adult world they were now moving in.

It had taken him a while of brooding and moodiness to get up the gumption to ask her out – though the way it had come about was less than courtly.

He'd been having a pint with Wes at the Rose & Crown when Chad had spotted Fallon emerge from the church hall with a young man at her side.

Wes had given him a nudge and laughed – at 17 he shouldn't have been drinking but he was going on 18 so Chad had bought the beer and brought it outside for him.

"Just look at that…" Wes had guffawed "…playing grown-ups." But when the lad at Fallon's side had pulled her to a halt and tried to kiss her, Wes hadn't found that funny at all. "What the hell?!"

He'd put his pint down and strode over to his sister, ready to beat the lad to dust for putting his hands on Fallon and was surprised when Chad beat him to it.

He had the boy by the front of his shirt, hauling him up to his toes. "If you want to live another minute you'd better apologise and then get yourself off home!"

Chad's voice had been quiet but lined with steal and a threat that had chilled the boy's blood.

"Yes. Yes. I will," the boy had agreed, nodding his head rapidly. He'd turned wide eyes to Fallon and said, "Sorry, I didn't think."

The moment Chad let the boy's feet touch the ground again, he was off like a greyhound out of the trap.

"What the hell were you thinking, letting that snivelling little runt kiss you like that?!" Wes growled out at his sister, who was coming out of her stupor and building up a head of temper.

"Don't you shout at me, Wesley Craemer!" Fallon told him, hands balled into tight fists resting on her hips. "He was only kissing me – I bet you've kissed a few girls in your time!"

"That's different," Wes had told her.

"Oh really – and that would be because you're a boy, I suppose?" Fallon asked, her temper simmering dangerously. When he nodded, she only smiled coldly. "But you were kissing a girl – if it's so wrong for me to be kissing someone then why isn't it wrong for those girls to be kissing you?!"

That flummoxed him for a moment, then Wesley turned to the time honoured words that his parents had sometimes fallen back on. "Because I said so!"

Fallon had stomped off, leaving Wesley to go back to his pint – but Chad had lost his taste for beer.

"Finish your pint…" he told Wes "…I'll make sure she gets home alright."

With that, he had left a stunned Wes outside the pub and had hightailed it after Fallon.

I should've known I was taking on a world of trouble then, Chad chuckled to himself as he pulled up at another locked gate. *But I wouldn't change a single thing about her – Fallon is her own woman and isn't afraid to tell anyone if she disagrees with them.*

He loved that about her. He loved the fire in her spirit, the depth of her passion and the way Fallon cared for the people she loved.

We'll be man and wife this time tomorrow, he thought wistfully as he relocked the gate he'd just driven the tractor through. *Christ, it's been a battle to get to this point, and I won't feel happy until we've said our 'I do's'. It won't feel real until it is real – signed and sealed, then the rest of our lives can begin.*

CHAPTER TWENTY-FOUR

The revelry began at 7 o'clock with Fenella handing out costumes to all the women now sat in her bedroom. "These are to get us into the spirit," she announced.

The wigs were made of tinsel in the brightest colours imaginable. Long strands fell straight to the shoulder and the fringe was cut blunt just above the eyes.

The dresses were very short with large checks in various colour combos. Pam's was pink and dark purple with a pink wig to match. Fallon wore deep gold and yellow with a yellow wig, Fenella had black and white checks with a silver wig, Ashton had blue and white with a white wig and Lizzy had green and white checks with a green wig.

They were all falling about laughing when they looked

at each other – especially Lizzy. "I've never seen anything like this before," she giggled, turning this way and that to see her reflection.

"It's a sixties theme night," Fenella told her. "Just wait till you see the dining room."

The girls all trooped downstairs, and when Fenella opened the doors to let them in the music bombarded their ears.

She had sixties music blaring out as a club scene played on the large pull down cine screen. Teenagers and young twenty somethings danced away dressed in clothes of a similar style to the ones the girls wore now.

The dining table had been moved against the wall and was laid out with finger foods and a whole range of alcoholic beverages and mixers.

A large banner hung on the wall over the table proclaiming, 'Hen do – Let's Party Hard!'.

Lit only by a revolving, multi-coloured sphere lamp, stood high on top of a bureau, Fenella moved onto what had been declared the dancefloor and started to boogie for all she was worth.

The rest of the girls gave a whoop and joined her, dancing like maniacs and thoroughly enjoying themselves.

"This is brilliant!" Ashton declared, shouting to be heard above the music. "The room looks great."

As well as the banner, Fenella had fetched out some Christmas trimmings and had used them to brighten the place up. Spots of light from the revolving lamp glanced off the tinsel garlands and gave the room a magical feel.

Their wigs also shimmered as they bobbed and shook their heads in time to the music.

When, at last, a slow Dianna Ross song came on, the girls all trooped over to the dining table to get welcome drinks.

"Phew, I must be out of shape," Pam declared, wiping her brow dramatically.

"It's the wigs," Ashton assured her. "I'm hot too."

But no one took the wigs off, they were having too much fun to care.

Thankfully everyone got themselves a plate of food as well as helping themselves to the drinks provided.

"Lizzy, you can have whatever you like," Ashton declared, and earned a worried frown from Pam. "This is a hen do, you can't stay sober at a hen do — it isn't allowed."

"Here, here," Fallon cheered in support, holding her glass of Bacardi and coke out in salute.

"Alright..." Lizzy said, gamely "...I'll have the same as you — it looks like pop, but I'm sure there's more to it."

Fallon laughed and got to her feet to fetch Lizzy a

Bacardi and coke but made it a bit weaker than her own.

"There you go, Lizzy, that'll help loosen you up," Fallon laughed.

It did. All the women were very loose by the time the alcohol had taken effect. They danced the evening away, eating and drinking as the mood took them then it was back on the dancefloor for more fun.

The men were having a less lively time of it, but were still managing to enjoy themselves.

Wesley was recounting some funny stories about the trouble they'd managed to get into as lads, and a few about Fallon to Chad's great surprise and merriment.

"I wasn't the least bit surprised when you two got together," Wes stated knowledgeably. "Fallon was always asking about you – used to doll herself up when she knew you were coming over."

Matt, Jackson and Mac all laughed at Chad's chagrined expression. "I doubt that very much," Chad rolled his eyes at Wes. "I had to virtually beg to get that first date – your sister is bloody hard work!"

Everyone laughed at that, including Chad.

"Marrying you though, isn't she lad." Mac raised his glass to Chad and winked.

"Christ, I had to whisk her off to Venice to convince her to do that," Chad told them, his tongue a bit loser now that he'd shared a glass or two of Mac's prime whiskey having already had a skin full of beer. "I still can't believe she finally said yes."

"I reckon she was just playing hard to get," Wes told him. "I know she was when you first started dating her – I heard her telling one of her mates she had staying over at the house."

"You never told me that!" Chad stared at his lifelong friend in shocked amazement.

"It was a bit embarrassing, tell the truth," Wes confessed, his voice beginning to slur. "I mean, she's my sister – I could hardly go around calling her a conniving female, now could I?"

"Not to all and sundry, no," Chad agreed with a frown. "But you could have told me – I might have handled things a bit differently if I'd known."

"And how would you have done that?" Matt asked, remembering how gone over Fallon his big brother had been. "You couldn't have played her at her own game, that's for sure. You were like a puppy at her heels."

The laughter was hearty and even Chad joined in. "Not quite…" he denied "…but at least I got the girl."

"So did I," Wesley grinned. "Had to wait for Ashton to grow up a bit, but she's mine now!"

They all raised their glasses in a toast. "To Fallon and

Ashton..." Matt said "...may they keep your beds warm and your stomachs full."

"To Fallon and Ashton," they all repeated, and clinked glasses together.

CHAPTER TWENTY-FIVE

The wedding day dawned bright and beautiful, the image of what every bride dreams of for her big day.

It was a bit on the chilly side yet, but then it was only 6 in the morning when Fallon found herself wandering around the paddock and stroking one of Fenella's horses.

"Hello, there," she crooned when the palomino moved closer to allow her to pet its head. "You're a beauty, you really are."

Stroking the velvet nose, Fallon wished she could have gone for a ride, there was nothing like it for clearing the head.

Hers was still a bit foggy, though she'd stopped adding Bacardi to her coke once she got the tell-tale tipsy feeling that told her she'd had enough. She hadn't wanted to get up with a hangover on her wedding day.

Not that that had stopped Ashton – she and Fenella had been joined at the hip and matched each other drink for drink.

Fenella seemed to be on manic overdrive – she'd danced and drunk the night away, laughing hysterically at every little thing.

Fallon had a feeling her friend's exuberance had more to do with trying to block out the upcoming events to do with her father than any real desire to party hard.

Lizzy had been pie-eyed and fell asleep on the settee in the sitting room. How they'd managed to get her to bed was anyone's guess, none of them had been very steady on their feet.

The one that had amazed Fallon was Pam – she'd never seen her friend so loose. She'd done a raunchy strip-tease number, having donned various items that were not all clothing. On top of tea towels draped over her shoulders, Pam had worn a cardigan and then a coat. Fenella had found some appropriately slutty music and Pam had done a provocative dance that saw her removing each item with great exaggeration.

Matt had no idea what he was missing, Fallon chuckled at the memory.

It had been a great night, Fallon couldn't deny that, couldn't help grinning at the memory of Ashton declaring her undying love for Wes before falling flat on her face in bed.

Yes, it had been a great party and Fallon wondered how the men had fared on their stag do.

Chad groaned as he pulled himself out of bed and made his way to the loo. He wasn't sick, thankfully, but his stomach felt jittery as he emptied his bladder of what was probably neat alcohol.

Why the hell had he drunk so much – did he want to be a stuttering, mumbling wreck at his own wedding?

Determined to get mind and body back together, he went downstairs with the intention of fuelling up on some very strong black coffee.

But when he walked into the sitting room Chad found Mac and Jackson sprawled out; Mac on the settee, one leg on one leg dangling off and Jackson's lanky frame was draped sideways over a matching armchair – he didn't look comfortable.

As it was 8 in the morning, Chad felt vindicated in waking the men up. "Mac, Jackson," he shouted as loudly as his head would allow, and gave them each a poke in the shoulder to rouse them. "I'm making coffee, you want?"

Both men groaned their assent and pulled themselves into an upright sitting position.

"Holy god, what happened to my head?" Jackson said, a hand to either side of it as if holding it on his shoulders.

Mac looked over at his son and smiled – yes, he actually smiled. "It's called a hangover, son. Not something I've ever suffered from, thank the Lord."

He didn't, Mac really didn't have a single sign of having polished off most of a bottle of whiskey. He looked like he'd had the best night's sleep a man ever did and Chad found it really annoying.

"What are you, a fucking robot?" Chad frowned deeply at the man who had taught him to ride a horse when he was a boy.

"Just blessed with a good constitution," Mac smiled annoyingly. "Now then, let me make that coffee while you sit down and recover a bit? I could make us all some bacon and eggs if you've got some in the fridge?"

That did it, Chad's jittery stomach clenched and he had to make a quick dash to the bathroom or show himself up by vomiting all over the sitting room floor.

"What did I say?" Mac asked no one in particular, but smiled roguishly as he took himself off to the kitchen.

It was a good job, all in all, that the wedding was set for 2 in the afternoon. Mac and Fallon were the only ones not struck down by hangovers and it would take them a few hours to get the others back on their feet.

By midday, everyone was feeling much better and most had even managed to eat and keep it down.

"You ready to don your shackles gents," Matt asked, grinning like a fool and jiggling his eyebrows at them. "I can tell you, mine fit perfectly – wouldn't change them for all the tea in china."

"And you love your tea," Mac said, handing Matt a mug full of fresh brew.

"You do seem suited to married life," Jackson commented as he polished off the bacon and eggs he'd finally felt able to eat. "You and Pam have never looked happier."

"I've seen you looking more content of late," Matt said, lifting a brow at Jackson. "Could that have anything to do with our neighbour, Fenella Swain?"

Not the least bit embarrassed, as Matt had hoped he would be, Jackson nodded and smiled. "It has everything to do with Fenella," he confirmed. "She's so damn brave over this impending court saga, you can't help but admire her for it."

"And you do so admire her," Matt grinned playfully.

"I do, yes, I really do," Jackson declared earnestly.

"Sounds serious," Chad put in, concerned for a man he now considered a friend. "You not worried about the differences between you – Fenella was born with a silver spoon in her mouth and seems to like the good life."

Jackson nodded, seemed to consider Chad's words before replying. "That's why I didn't ask her out for quite a while – I wasn't sure we'd be a good fit. But we've talked about it and Fenella isn't bothered that I don't have the millions her daddy does, most of which will likely be appropriated as ill-gotten-gains after he's convicted in a court of law."

"You're sure he will be?" Mac asked, also concerned for his son as he'd heard a lot about the way Theodore Swain operated.

"Oh yes, there isn't a doubt about it," Jackson told them, sitting back in his chair. "I saw the evidence Fenella found before I went with her to hand it over to the police – Swain won't wriggle his way out of a prison cell, that's a certainty."

"It's going to be rough on her," Matt observed. "I don't want you to worry about going with her when Fenella has to make a court appearance or this interview deal she has coming up in London – you're a damned hard worker, Jackson, I'll see to it that you get full pay."

He had to swallow hard on the emotions that welled in his throat, but Jackson managed to say a few words. "I really appreciate that. I've been saving hard to get a place of my own – Fenella and I took a walk around those houses you built and she took a shine to one of them," he smiled shakily. "She isn't as mercenary as some people think – Fenella just wants to be accepted, cared for as any other woman would want to be."

"Then I hope it works out for you, son." Mac clapped a hand on Jackson's back and nodded. "We'll talk about that house later – for now, we have to get these two fine men into their wedding suits and get them to the church on time."

Everyone laughed as Mac sang the last few words to the old song, then collected up their dishes and piled them in the kitchen.

The girls looked beautiful in their very short wedding dresses. Each had chosen to rebel against the traditional long gowns and had picked out the most outrageous, but gorgeous, dresses they could find.

Dressed in her powder blue bridesmaids dress, Lizzy looked at them with envy and pride. "You look so beautiful," she told them, her round eyes trying to take in every detail.

Fallon and Ashton looked at each other and nodded in agreement. "May not be what the men are expecting..." Fallon chuckled happily "...but I think they'll like what they're getting just fine."

"They better had," Ashton laughed. "It took me forever to get my hair tamed even this much, and my arms are aching like hell."

"I said I'd help you," Pam put in as she came into the

bedroom where the brides were getting ready. "But you did a good job – Wes will love that you left most of your hair down, I know he likes it that way."

"Oh, and how's that?" Ashton asked, interested in her sister-in-laws observation.

"I've seen the way he looks at you, the way he strokes your hair and gets that dreamy look in his eyes," Pam smiled.

Ashton actually blushed, Wes had told her exactly what he was thinking about when he got 'that look' and it wouldn't bare repeating in the current company.

"I don't know what you mean," she lied smoothly, but everyone laughed and Ashton had to accept that she hadn't pulled it off. "Well, anyway, hadn't we better be leaving soon," she said, trying to turn the attention away from herself.

Fenella looked at her wrist watch and nodded. "You're right – I'll ask Charley to make sure the limo driver is ready to go." With that, Fenella went off and left the brides and bridesmaids to enjoy a moment alone.

"This is it," Fallon laughed nervously.

Pam passed both girls each a little posy of white roses with powder blue ribbons woven through them. Then they all turned to the mirrored wardrobes that lined Fenella's bedroom and gazed at the picture they made.

"I can barely believe you two pulled all this off in just a

month, but you did," Pam smiled happily. "I'm so happy I just might cry, only we don't have time to redo my make-up."

"That's right…" Fallon turned to hug her lifelong friend "…so let's just get moving and go downstairs."

Charley was stood at the bottom of the large staircase in the main foyer and watched the girls descend.

His eyes filled with shock at first then quickly turned to pride. "You all look stunning," he told the group of women as they came to stand beside him. "Different, but then I should have expected that," Charley said, playfully rolling his eyes at his daughter.

"That's what we were going for," Ashton agreed, then reached up to give her father a hug. "I love you, daddy."

Charley felt his throat choke up but managed to swallow back the emotions that threatened to swamp him and gave Ashton a hug in return.

Then he looked at Lizzy, standing back still a little shy of him. "And look at you two lovely ladies," he said, looking at Pam and Lizzy. "Do a twirl so I can get a better look at you."

Doing as they were told, Pam and Lizzy turned a full circle then looked back at Charley.

"Lovely, absolutely lovely," Charley declared. "I hardly recognise you, Lizzy. I don't think I've ever seen you in a dress before – quite the grown up young lady."

Blushing prettily, Lizzy thanked him shyly.

When the limo driver knocked at the door, Charley went to answer it.

"Ok, ladies, this is it. The car is out front and ready to go," he told them.

Fenella was travelling to the church with Jackson, who was parked at the back of the white stretched limousine. "Don't forget to enjoy your big day," she told both brides as they all moved outside. "I've been told it can go by in a blink and you want to remember every moment."

It might be just a register office that they were going to, but for both brides this was a momentous and thrilling occasion.

The men were already there – Chad was nervously pacing back and forth while Wes was getting his tie straightened by Mac – he'd been so nervous, Wes had all but undone it during the journey from the farm.

"Stand still, lad," Mac told him when he ended up having to undo the tie and start again. "Your future wife is going to be here any minute and she won't be too happy if you look like you just crawled out of bed."

When Wes hadn't been fidgeting with his tie he'd been running his hands through his hair and had turned it into a blond mop.

"Ok, that's the tie sorted, now give your hair a comb," Mac told him.

But Wes didn't have a comb on him and looked franticly at Chad who just shrugged and shook his head.

"Good grief, the pair of you look like you're going to the gallows instead of getting married," Mac told them. "Here, use mine," and he handed Wes a comb from his jacket pocket.

The registrar smiled patiently having seen all this before, many times. "Gentlemen, if you'd like to take your places, I've just been informed that the brides have arrived and are on their way in."

Avis and Sheila were sat together on the second row, and waited expectantly for their daughters to make their entrance into the room.

The florist had done a wonderful job of the flowers and the office actually looked like a wedding was about to take place.

Jackson and Fenella came into the room first, taking their seats next to Mac and on the same row as Avis and Sheila. Then, moments later, both brides entered together, followed by their bridesmaids.

Wes and Chad were stood at the front of the room and both wore identical expressions. Their eyes were round, their jaws dropped and neither one could string a coherent thought together.

The two brides smiled at each other, acknowledging that they had achieved their goal.

Moving next to Wesley, Ashton took his hand in hers and gave it a squeeze. "You like…?" she asked softly.

All Wesley could do was nod enthusiastically and Ashton let out a satisfied giggle.

Next to them Fallon looked up at Chad and simply waited, a sexy smile playing over her delicately painted lips.

"I think I must have died and gone to heaven," Chad moaned into Fallon's ear as he bent to her. "You look exquisite."

It turned out that Fenella had been right – no matter how Fallon and Ashton tried to hang on to every moment of their special day, it passed by in a blink.

They thanked their lucky stars that they had given in to the tradition of having a wedding photographer and would no doubt enjoy countless hours reminiscing over their photos.

They hadn't needed the big church or a splashy wedding with lots of guests; close family and friends, and all the love they brought with them, had been enough.

*****

If you have enjoyed this book, please leave a review at the place of purchase. Thank you.

www.ingramcontent.com/pod-product-compliance
Lightning Source LLC
Chambersburg PA
CBHW070627170726
48291CB00003B/908